Crystal's Method

Crystal's Method

A Domestic
Violence Novel

Jaz Cyan

In memory of my grandmother
1954-2002

In memory of my great grandmother
1922-2003

In memory of Bobby Rogers
1940-2013

"Pain touches every life, but if you're open, it will also teach you a valuable life lesson."

— SARAH JAKES ROBERTS

PROLOGUE
MAY 2022

I STARE AT THE frame hanging beside the door. From where I am sitting, I can see it clearly. Except I am not really looking at it. This is just my latest attempt to avoid the person in front of me.

Not that she is intimidating. No. In fact, she has a mothering demeanor I find very endearing. Maybe that's why I chose her as my new therapist. After meeting almost all the therapists in this office and being the client of two of them already, this might be my final switch. I like her energy.

If only I could bring myself to just open up to her more. I've told her so much already, though.

I can feel her looking at me. She does this thing where she doesn't speak but still communicates. Letting me know the channel is open for me to speak.

She chuckles lightly. "I don't know why I still leave their picture up there. It's way too distracting for a therapist's office decor, right?"

I shake my head and lift up the edges of my lips in a smile. "I don't think so." I stare again at what seems to be a picture from the famous *Lion King* scene, where Simba, a cub, is being presented to the animals in the kingdom. There he was. All innocent and happy.

Poor Simba. If only he knew what life had in store for him.

Kinda like me, I guess.

I close my eyes and take a deep breath and finally turn to face Dr. Andrews.

"I'm ready to answer your questions," I say to her.

She nods slightly but takes a few seconds before speaking.

"So tell me, Crystal, how does it affect you today?"

My lips start to quiver. I shrug while looking upward, fighting back tears.

How can such a simple question feel so heavy?!

I shake my head to try and dial back the tears as memories come flooding in. Memories I thought I buried, swirling through my head like a movie, bringing along with them the heavy weight of emotions that almost crushed me–

"Breathe, Crystal." I hear Dr. Andrews' voice seep into my mind. She feels so far away even though she is sitting just a few feet in front of me. "In," she guided, "and out." I follow her directions and start to feel better.

A few minutes later, calmer, I close my eyes and finally answer her question. Making the admission with a bitter chuckle.

"I don't—I don't know!" I shrug my shoulders to emphasize my answer.

"Can you tell me what you think about it?" she asks.

This time, I cannot help the tears as they fall. I quickly reach for a tissue from the box in front of me and dab my eyes. "Oh, that is a long story, Doc."

"It's a good thing we got time, then." Dr. Andrews leans back and taps her pen lightly on the pad on her lap. "Why don't you start from the beginning, Crystal?"

CHAPTER ONE
ADOLESCENT ... WITH DADDY ISSUES: DETROIT, MI, 2000

"I THINK YOU GOT them 'Daddy Issues,' Crystal," Nelly says as I stand over her, watching a father pick up one of our classmates after our dance rehearsal. Nelly is sitting on the floor, tying her shoes.

"What does that mean?" I ask her.

"It's like when someone who doesn't have a dad and then has problems and like really wants one and stuff. I heard my mom talking about it the other day," Nelly responds, trying to sound smarter than she is.

She loved this. Finding a reason to tell me new stuff, even though most times she doesn't know what she's talking about, but considers herself "the cultured one."

"You're doing it again, Crystal!" Nelly whines and brings me back to the present.

"Doing what?"

"That thing you do where you go blank and start thinking of things in your head."

"Oh–"

"My mama always says it's better to have your feet on the ground than in your head."

"Yes. Yes, I was just thinking about—uhh—nothing."

"Hmm-mm." Nelly rolls her eyes. Obviously, she is not buying my clumsy response. She pulls her left foot up to tie her shoe while examining the dirt on the shoelaces.

But I don't care if she believes me or not. I have to figure out a way to get Nelly to tell me more about this "Daddy Issue" thing she mentioned earlier. This may be the closest I get to figuring it out.

"But I have a father," I respond almost immediately in an irritated tone, grating on impatience.

She knows I have a father, not one I know or remember, but I do have one … somewhere. I really don't know where Nelly is going with this. Does having "Daddy Issues" imply that I don't have a father or more about me dressing up my alternate life if I had a present father doing all the daddy stuff? Like her stepfather.

"Not like a real one that's around and all that. Do you even remember what your pops look like?"

I can't argue with that. It's been so long that I have forgotten his face. "So, does this mean that you have daddy issues too?"

"No. My daddy died. It's not possible to have daddy issues with a dead father. He didn't leave me on purpose. Besides, I got Walter now. He's a great guy." Nelly jumps to her feet. "Daddy issues are for people like you."

I scrunched my face, annoyed, trying to follow that logic. I know she does not intend to be mean, but I cannot help being sad. I mean, I am happy for her. That she has someone like Dr. Walter who loves her. But I still do not like this 'daddy issues' explanation. And you know what? Maybe Nelly doesn't know what she is talking about. Just because her stepfather is a doctor doesn't mean she knows everything. In fact, I am pretty sure he doesn't know everything. But I can't tell Nelly that. She idolizes the man.

"Let's go get ice cream. I'll tell you more about it," Nelly suggests.

"I have to go to my grandmother's place. My mom started evening classes at the community college."

"Yeah, right after we get some ice cream. I've got money. Let's go!" Nelly grabs my arm and playfully pulls me off the short step into the street. "We're having a barbecue later tonight. There is no way I'll be able to sneak some ice cream with that many people in the house."

"Sure," I grudgingly agree and grab my backpack. "You guys are having a lot of weekend barbecues these days."

Nelly rolls her eyes, but there is a smile at the end of it. "Yeah, I know. It's almost every weekend now. I like it, though. Walter has a big family, and all of a sudden, I have a lot of cousins. I'll introduce you to some of them when you come around."

Nelly has been my best friend since kindergarten. Her full name is Penelope, but she freaks if anyone dares to call her that. She says she hates the way it is pronounced. I think it is a cool name. She doesn't care about that, though. It is *Nelly* to everyone in the world, even her mother.

Our bond is simple. We were always the last on the playground when we were younger. This was because our mothers were always the last to pick us up. When you grow up in Detroit, where almost everyone has to get two jobs while still struggling to make ends meet, it is not unusual to have busy parents who cannot make it to the school on time to pick up their kids.

So, we kept each other company. Imagining ourselves as princesses that lived in castles. It wasn't hard to picture. Not because we saw a lot of real-life black princesses—which we didn't—we just always felt this inner pride that we were two pretty, black girls that should definitely be princesses and live in castles. Honestly, I don't know where that pride came from.

Our parents—both single mothers—were barely making a living despite all the hours they worked. Didn't matter; we always felt like we were meant for the castle life. We spent most of our time thinking up scenarios that made us royal. It was ridiculous, but I would do anything to feel like that again. Like the world belonged to me. So yes, that is me and Nelly, my first real friend. We have known each other the longest, so I am sure she knows what she is talking about. That doesn't mean she is right, though; at least that is what I think.

Nelly has always been one to speak her mind, not caring what you make of it. She will leave the chaos in her wake if it means that the truth gets out there. Her mother is the same. Perhaps that was why our mothers didn't get along. I think my mother felt judged by Nelly's mom, who is a widow and did not intentionally put herself in a position where she was raising her child alone, unlike my mother, who had fallen for a dreamer—at least that's what she calls him. My father abandoned us when I was a baby because he couldn't be "held down." I think my mother threw him out, though. Maybe it was when she discovered he had gotten another woman pregnant while she was pregnant. I mean, I have a half-sister who is six months younger than me. Explain that!?

One time I saw our mothers almost like each other. My mom had come to pick me up earlier than *usual* because she got off early. All through that day, Nelly was feeling off, and she complained about something being wrong with her stomach. So, when my mom came, I quickly took her hand and told her something was wrong. She pulled her phone out and tried to call Nelly's mom, but it was not going through. She kept trying and finally was able to get her, but she said she was still at work and it may take her about thirty minutes to make the commute, so instead, my mom offered to take Nelly to the ER. We had to wait, and my mom had to raise her voice at a nurse that kept asking rude, insensitive questions, even though Nelly's mom had supplied all the necessary information over the phone. Nelly's mom must've heard my mama yelling because when she finally came to the hospital after Nelly had to be admitted for food poisoning, they grabbed each other as if they were holding on for dear life. Well, maybe it did not make them friends, but it did make them more understanding of each other's struggles. Three years later, when Nelly's mom got married again, to a doctor, we were invited to the wedding. My mom did not want to be there. She only attended because I got to wear a beautiful dress along with Nelly when we walked down the aisle as junior bridesmaids. My mom was very uncomfortable being there, but she kept a smile plastered on her face; Trisha Branson would never be caught without her manners.

If only she could also have that type of pride in her body. She keeps giving it to nonsense, good-for-nothing men who end up leaving her or even hurting her.

Ever since I was a child, it has been one bad decision after another. Sometimes, I would overhear her and my grandmother having heated conversations about her way of life. And most times, the controversy is usually around the type of men my mother dated.

Last year, my mom went out a few times with DeVante, a famous drug dealer in our city. Everyone knew DeVante and stayed away from him. But not Trisha, obviously. And when my grandmother got wind of it, they argued for days. Whatever my grandmama said must've worked because I stopped seeing DeVante around my mother.

My dad left when I was very young. I don't remember his face or even remember loving him. It's hard to say I miss him because I don't think that is completely true. I do miss having a father and have always wondered if my life would be easier with a father. Maybe even help my mama out with the bills, but I never let myself dwell too much on that because even though she has never complained about having me, sometimes I wonder why she did. I don't see her as lonely either because she never cared, either way, about my dad.

The last time I saw him was four years ago. He had pulled up to my school on a huge motorcycle. He breezed in and out of town before I could even form a memory of him.

The phrase "Daddy Issues" is now in almost every one of Nelly's sentences. It's easier to accept than to fight it. Maybe one day, I will let her know how I really judge whenever she calls me out with my "Daddy Issues."

"We should get the Monkey Crunch," Nelly suggests, drawing me out of my musing.

"Yeah, yeah, sure!" I respond, even though I hate Monkey Crunch. But I am too distracted to think of anything else; not even ice cream flavors are good enough to get my mind off this recent episode of "Daddy Issues" Nelly has come up with.

If he was here, maybe the creepy thing that happened this morning would not have happened. And I would not still be feeling dirty and exposed–

Maybe I can ask my grandmother later tonight—or not. I am not sure I want to ever talk about it. Maybe if I never say anything, I can make myself believe it never happened. And I know if I tell my grandmother, she will blame my mom. Their relationship is dicey already. This could be what breaks it. I know there is no way my grandmother would let it go that my mom was in the house when it happened. And even though I cannot bring myself to explain what I am feeling toward my mother yet, I do know that it will break my mother's heart if I tell my grandmother first. It's just better all-around that I keep this to myself. I just have to think of a way to make sure I never see Sean again.

We continue walking without talking, too busy licking the ice cream as it drips down our fingers. We normally ride our bicycles, but not today. After dance class, our legs are usually too tired to pedal our bikes, so just walking becomes a better option.

"So, what do we tell Danielle?" Nelly asks when we are almost done.

Danielle is our best friend. She lives at the other end of our block. We don't get to see each other often, especially because she doesn't take dance class with us. She is in the choir group of the community program that also organizes the dance class that we attend. She cannot dance to save her life but has the voice of an angel. She did try to audition for the dance squad, but she struggled so much that she started hiding in the bathroom for most of the rehearsals until one of the tutors heard her singing and encouraged her to join the choir, which she now loves. But it just means that we don't get to hang out together as much.

She is always sensitive about missing out on all the fun, so we like to tease her about all the "fun" things we do, which mostly doesn't happen. Usually, we intentionally exaggerate to pull her leg.

"I think we should tell her we got to taste all the flavors before we settled on three cones, which we ate till our brains froze!" Nelly pipes in as her eyes dance in mischief.

I burst out laughing. "She would die!"

"Serves her right for being able to hit those great runs like Whitney Houston."

"I can't wait for their showcase." I jump in glee, my eyes glistening as Nelly stares at me, wondering why I am so interested in the choir showcase. Everyone knows that the dance showcase attracts more attention.

I roll my eyes when she still doesn't get it. "There will be seventh graders there!" I remind her.

Seeing as she still looks clueless. I open my eyes wider as I add, "Antwon!" I say in what is supposed to be a whisper but is definitely not. "Antwon is going to be there!"

We are obviously boy-crazy, and we prefer to obsess over seventh graders. It's hard to like boys you have known since kindergarten. Seventh graders are more mysterious to us. But my girls and I had our crushes already.

"Girl, please!" she shot back. "Antwon ain't even fine. Devon? Now, *he* is dreamy."

"Devon? Dreamy? Come on!" I stare at her in disbelief as if she has grown two heads. Devon is barely visible under those huge glasses he wears. And he is not finer than Antwon. The prettiest boy in school?! What is Nelly saying right now?!

We argue until we get to my grandmother's apartment building, stopping only to get our stories straight to make Danielle jealous the next day at school. We had to plot about how to get her to objectively pick the more handsome boy between Devon and Antwon to finally settle our disagreement. I will have to make sure I convince Danielle to let us do a quick walk-by when Antwon is on his way to his homeroom class. Smiling and saying hello to everyone. Danielle will see that Antwon is clearly unmatched.

Nelly and I hug, and I wave her off. She turns and skips down the road to her house, which is just after the next stop sign.

I make my way up inside the apartment. My grandmother's place is just on the fourth floor, so it is not much of a journey. There is an elevator, but it's so old and creaky that no one who had legs would dare use it. Even if the building wasn't old, I wouldn't use it today. I need time to think as I climb the stairs. I really don't know whether to tell my grandma about this.

Something happened, and I don't even know if it is a thing.

I can't tell my mama.

Her current boyfriend, Sean, has stuck around longer than usual. They dated about two years ago but broke up when I saw a busted lip on my mom. And now, they are back together, and I do not know how to tell her that Sean scares me, and I usually feel like screaming every time I see him ... or he sees me. Like he did this morning.

My mom had slept in this morning, so I got up early to prepare for school. I was in the bathroom daydreaming while taking a bath when I heard a muffled but shallow breath behind me. I instantly knew it was not my mother. My flesh ran cold. I sat still, held my breath, and shut my eyes hard. Hoping it was a dream and that it was all in my head ... that ... that there was no grown man standing behind me, watching me bathe.

After some seconds of hesitance, I turned my neck around slowly to see him standing there, staring at me with his eyes almost shut but disturbingly alert with a crooked smile on his face. And as my eyes went down, I saw a huge bulge in his boxers, and he had his hand moving suspiciously. It seemed like I lost my voice; I could not scream even though I wanted to, desperately. It was as if his eyes had been daring me to. I sat there like a deer in headlights, panting heavily as his hands moved faster inside his boxers. His eyes seemed to glaze over as a growl escaped his lips like a wild animal.

Then he took his hand out, covered in a thick white liquid. He looked at his hands and then winked at me before turning to leave.

For a minute, I just sat there. In shock. Still mortified, shaking so hard I had to wrap my hands around myself. I started to scrub my skin as hard as I could as if that would wash his gaze off me. It's like I was in a trance. I poured water on my body and went about the mechanics of getting ready for school, grabbing my lunch money, and meeting up with Nelly to walk to school.

My grandma is not on duty at the hospital today, so I know she is home, but I still use my key to open the door. She is not the type to come open the door for anyone except if the person is Denzel Washington, she says.

I open the door, push it in, and step inside. The scent always hits me like a surprise. You would think I'd be used to it by now. The strong aroma of something cooking or cooling and the combination of antiques and several homemade cleaning agents make me feel like I am home. Sometimes, I wish my mom would just stop being proud and let us move in with my grandmother.

I feel more at home here than in our own apartment. The walls in the hallway are filled with my pictures and just a few other relatives. I walk into my grandma's sitting room with the brown leather sofa that dominates the space looking worn but dignified. They are adorned with some handmade, beautiful embroidery that I love. She always said she would one day teach me how to make them as her mama taught her. She tried to teach my mother, but she never cared to learn. No surprise there. This is definitely not my mother's speed. I don't even think they could spend an hour alone together without raising their voices in disagreement.

But I love being with her, in her time. Doing the things

she loves and enjoys makes me feel like I am instantly as wise as her. She calls me an old soul. I don't understand why. Everything I know and do, I learned from her. My grandmother gives all the education about our culture and our family. "Family" includes all the black people she knows and a few famous people she has met.

I love listening to her stories. How her entire body rocks when she laughs, or how she gets all small and distant when she tells the several stories of tensions in Detroit back then, or when she was discriminated against as a black nurse. She loves to tell the story of how she and her friends traveled to march with Rev. Martin Luther King Jr. after he gave his "I Have a Dream" speech in Washington, D.C., in 1963, when she was still in college. How they took care of several people that were injured in the Twelfth Street riot in July 1967. She tells these stories like she is reliving them. And I feel like I am right there with her.

She sometimes tells me about when jazz bands came into town. She and her friends would put on their shimmering outfits, which was the rave back then, and go out dancing from midnight till morning, enjoying the adoring eyes that looked on as they sometimes took their rehearsed moves to the dance floor. They even managed to get a rare picture with the legendary artist, Miles Davis, who was so impressed by them when he came to perform at a club in Detroit.

Oh, I love that story and the ones about how when she used to go watch her long-time friend, Bobby Rogers, teach choreography to the Hall of Fame singing group, "The Miracles." Bobby Rogers is also a singer and songwriter in their group. She listens to their music so much that when I come over, I've learned many of their lyrics. The way she tells the stories about them and her friend Bobby sounds like she has a crush on him, but I never ask. When their famous song "Love

Machine" comes on, she always smiles and says, "Listen to that sexy growl!" when he says, "*Ooooooyeah*" during the chorus. I just laugh and keep singing along with her.

Funny how her skin glows in her sixties, but she has an almost full head of gray hair.

She lost her husband very young. My grandfather fought in the Vietnam War and died in the 1968 Tet Offensive. That's as much as I know about him except for pictures I've seen. I asked her about him once, and she politely brushed it off while not answering the question, so I never ask anymore. She had only been married two years when he died, and my mama was just a baby. I think she loved him so much that even though it had been over thirty years, she still struggled to bring him up. I sometimes wished she would talk about him when she got into her interesting stories of how Detroit used to be home to jazz and how much fun she used to have "back in her day." But she was never one to bring things down. She took care of everyone, and everything had a story. Just like her Phonograph and her precious records. She made me love jazz and rock 'n' roll.

"Dreaming again, Crystal?" I hear her call from behind me. I turn around and see her poking her head out from the kitchen.

I chuckle and turn around. "Yes, Grandma." There is no use lying; she knows me too well.

"That's well and good. Keep that sharp mind working. You're going to do great things, my dear girl. I am making some lasagna for the new family that just moved into the building—Bakers—that's their name. I'm making us something else. Go drop your backpack and come help."

"Okay."

"Your mama dropped by with a change of clothes for you.

She has a study group this evening and will be here to pick you up tomorrow morning."

I walk into the second bedroom, which doubles as my room whenever I stay over. I have my pajamas here as well as my toiletries and some clothes. So even if my mama had not dropped off new ones, I would still have fresh, clean clothes for school—and church.

I put my backpack on the bed and changed my shoes to a pair of slippers that my mama leaves here for me before making my way back to the kitchen.

I sniff the air and jump in delight. "Salmon Croquettes!" I scream as I run to put my hand around her waist and hug her from the side.

She laughs and turns a little to kiss my head. She is my favorite person, and she knows it. "You're welcome, honey. Come help with the rice and corn."

I put on the petite apron that she bought for me on my eighth birthday when I could finally see her kitchen counter without the stool. I was so proud of my spurt.

I grab some corn and start peeling it off the cob. This is the best kind!

"Be careful, dear. Stay alert, so you don't cut yourself."

I helped peel the corn a few months back, and I completely forgot how she taught me to hold the corn and the knife and nearly cut my thumb off. I know what she means, so I nod my head in understanding as she smiles.

We work in silence for a few minutes. Before I blurt out a question that has been on my mind for so long. "Do you think my mama is happy?"

It must have come as a surprise because she stops what she is doing but takes a few seconds before looking at me with a shaky smile. "Do you think she is unhappy?"

I shrug. "I don't know. I sometimes wish I knew what is on her mind."

"Well, honey, you cannot. But you just have to trust that she loves you so much and she is doing all she can to provide a good life for you."

"Hmm." I just nod and continue peeling. She knows I am not satisfied with that answer.

"Do you think her life would be different if she had not had me?"

"What? Why would you ever say that?"

"Nothing. Nothing, I just sometimes watch her struggle, and I feel bad. Like maybe if she never had me, she would not be raising a child alone, working two jobs, and taking evening classes–"

"No," she cuts me off. "Your mother loves you."

She takes a deep breath before admitting. "You know something? She wanted you even when I did not."

"I don't understand."

"I hoped I would never tell you this because I know she never would. But I think you are old enough to know the truth." She exhaled deeply, her eyes sad as if she was about to get crucified. This is a new emotion for my grandma. Now I am worried almost as much as curious with what she is about to say.

She finally speaks in a low tone. Not looking me in the eye. "You see, honey, even though I eventually came around when your mother first told me she was pregnant, I was against the idea of her keeping you."

She pauses, and I wait for her to continue.

"She was young and still figuring out what to do with her life. And maybe I was not the best mother to her. After my Morris died, I had to raise her alone. She loved to dance, and even when I did not understand it, I tried to hide my disapproval. And failed. She rebelled, and we fought. A lot. Then she left home to join a dance group that traveled through several towns. Can you imagine how that must have looked?" She shook her head and sighed. "I tried to be patient, hoping she would outgrow that phase and finally figure out what she wanted for her life." She smiled shakily as her eyes filled. "One day, just out of the blue, I heard a knock on my door." She pauses again. This time she stops what she is doing and stares at the door. As if she is reliving the day she heard this knock. "I heard a knock on the door," she says again in a hushed tone. "Your mother was pregnant. She told me the news, and I was not sure whether she was ready to be a mother, so I advised her to get rid of the pregnancy." She closes her eyes and sighs in relief. "She refused. Told me she knew this child was her destiny. That she was going to have her baby anyway, with or without my support. No amount of threat and cajoling worked. Your mother's mind was made up."

When she finally turns to look at me, her eyes are filled with tears. "But then you came along. All tiny feet and gorgeous. Just like your mother. And you brought so much joy to our lives. You have brought so much joy into MY life." She comes around the counter and puts her hands on my face.

"Your mother fought for you, my dear. She wanted to be your mother more than anything. And she is trying to make a better life for the both of you. She may not show it as you would like, but you, Crystal, mean the world to her. Do you know why she named you 'Crystal'?"

I shake my head "no" in response.

"Because no jewel in the world is as pure or beautiful as you. One look into your eyes, and she decided to name you Crystal. You are precious, my child. And you are going to do great things. Never forget that." She pulls me close to her bosom and hugs me tight. "You are precious," she says again.

"But why does my daddy not want me? He never comes. How come he never comes, Gran Gran?" I wet her clothes with my tears as she just rubs my back, letting me cry as much as I want.

"Oh, my child. I wish I had the answers for you. But sometimes, we don't know. And we have to live with the fact that we may never know."

She pulls me back and wipes my tears with her hand. "Come."

She makes her way to the sitting room and pulls out a letter from the middle of her favorite Billie Holiday record.

"One day. I will let you read this." She holds the old envelope up to me. "Not today, though. But when you are older, remind me to let you read this. I will keep it, and on your twenty-fifth birthday, you get to read it."

She takes a seat and asks me to sit with her. "Instead, I will tell you a bit about your grandfather." She smiled dreamily. "His name was Morris. Morris Branson. And he was the loveliest man in all of Detroit. Oh, he swept me off my feet with just one look. The day I met him, I had woken up late and was trying to catch a bus in the rain to go to class. I had just started college, and it was driving me crazy. My head was down as I ran, so when I got close to the bus, I almost pushed him over as he approached from the other side. And so, both drenched, we just stood there staring at each other until the driver yelled, and we climbed onto the bus. I took off my coat and sat down when he came to sit beside me. I cannot even remember what we talked about. Just a bunch of meaningless things. But he made me laugh and smile. I have never felt so light and giggly and–"

I stare as she pauses and gazes at nothing. Her mind has been transported.

"He played the trumpet. He was so good too. He was in a band ... 'The Moonstruck' ... 'Stupid name,' I told him. He chuckled and said, 'It makes us dreamy.' And they were. They struck their chords and pulled at your heartstrings. I would go to the club and watch him play. He would wink at me between half-closed eyes, and I would feel like the luckiest girl in the room. Morris got me, you know! He knew days when I wanted to just sit by the river and watch the small waves. He knew when I wanted to dance the night away. He knew when I was angry about the discrimination I faced in college. He knew, and somehow, we just fit. We fit. He was my person."

She pauses again to wipe a tear from her eyes as she places the words close to her chest.

"He was not much of a talker, but he wrote so beautifully. His words were so pure and honest. The year I graduated and became a nurse, we went out to celebrate, and that was when he told me he had signed up for the army. I told him it was a stupid war, not for our people. But he said he wanted to do something. 'Be an American,' he said. Make his mark. Do his duty. Wanted to prove himself. He–"

Another weighty pause.

"He signed up and was sent to Vietnam. He finished his first tour and came back. We did not want to wait any longer. We got married. He gave me the most beautiful wedding. Made me the happiest bride in the world. Oh, I loved him so much. I even managed as much as I could to send him back to war with a smile on my face after begging him not to leave me again, and he refused. He left again, saying, 'the war would be over soon' and 'Nixon would end the war.' And just when we thought the worst was over and things were finally turning around, expecting my Morris would return to me and we would happily be together forever, he died. 'In combat,' they said. And then they returned what was left of his body, which was nothing but a few mementos. He died, and for the longest time, I could not grieve because I was so angry. Why did he leave me? Why did he join the army? Even when I begged him not to?" She holds out the letter in her hand again. It looks … clearly old.

"This was the last letter he wrote before he died. He did not even get the chance to postmark it. They sent it to me as a part of his belongings. I did not want to open it, but when I did, I saw that he was human. Not the perfect man I hoped. He was human, and he had his battles. Everyone is going through something, and sometimes it has nothing to do with you and does not mean they love you any less. Then I grieved. I was so broken, and by then, I already had your mama. To be honest, I do not think I was the best mama to her. I tried to be, but I was struggling a lot and did not find myself as giving as I should've been …

"So, Crystal. I don't know where your father is or why he is not here. But I know you cannot live your life wondering about what drives people to make the decisions they make. Instead, you can look around you and appreciate the people that love you with purity and are here with you. Because in the end, that is all that matters. Those people you can count on to not hurt you are the ones that matter. Don't ever forget that."

"Yes, Gran Gran." I nod and wrap my arms around her shoulders as she pulls me into a deep embrace.

I have always wanted to hear that story. And it is sadder than I expected. Although I don't know if I will ever love as intensely as my grandmother speaks about, but I hope to God it doesn't end in tears.

Chapter Two
A New Bloom: 2002

I LOVE THE FALL season …

There is a light drizzle outside as I look through the window of my last class for the day. It's a geography class, and while on normal days, I would usually pay enough attention to Mrs. Williams' teaching, today, I'm very distracted.

Something is wrong. I can feel it. And it bothers me so much that I don't know what it is. My mama says it is just intuition, but my grandma tells me I have a gift. My grandma calls it *"the feels."* She says there is no explanation. Just like when she has one of her dreams. She dreams about something, and then it happens! How do you explain that?!

I live with my grandma now. I had moved back in with her this year before school started. My mama has two new jobs; one waiting tables at a restaurant during the day, and the second, in a crooked bar in the evenings. She says my grandmother will do better keeping an eye on me, but we both know that is not the reason. Even though I never told her or anyone what happened a long time ago with Sean, I have always felt like she noticed the change in me. How I flinched whenever I was around him, how I never even wanted to be around him, how I never let any part of my skin show ... She must have known something and was too scared to ask me. She broke up with Sean a month after the incident, but I was surprised when one morning, my mother asked me, "So, Crystal, I want to ask Gran Gran about you going to school from her place. Is that something you would like?"

I could not believe my ears ... Finally! But I managed to contain my joy so my mother would not feel bad. And it was settled.

I remember the first day I moved in, my grandmother pulled me into her bosom and whispered, "You're home. You're safe here." I held on to her warm embrace and allowed myself to breathe easily. I burst into tears. All I could think about was that morning with Sean. I did not tell her anything, but she cried with me. For a long time, we just stayed like that as she whispered over and over that sentence that I hold onto like a lifeline, "You're safe here."

When I first moved in, my mama dropped by every Saturday, or on her days off, to eat dinner with us. We would all cook together, and I would let myself believe for just a few hours that maybe ... I have a resemblance to a real family. But all that changed when she got a new boyfriend, Titus.

The first day I met him, my mama had walked me home from school after she had missed dinner the night before. I could almost sense she was on something. She was jumpy and light and almost just as scared at the same time. Since she was in a happy mood, I decided not to give her *a hard time* for not being at dinner. We even seemed to be having a nice conversation about some of our old neighbors when a car pulled up beside us. In a split second, my mother grabbed and pulled me behind her, her hand pushing my head back as I tried to peek at the driver of the car. Her body started to shiver as she tried to fake enthusiasm over his questions.

After confirming that she would be going home soon and would have the dinner ready, the car drove away. Just like that, I knew that my mother had gotten herself into another situation.

This time, I even fear it will be worse than Sean. And now more than ever, I am so grateful to not have to live with her.

Weeks after that day, she barely came around. She quit her job and started rolling around with Titus and his crew, who my grandmother believes are dealing drugs and distributing them through the neighborhood. More people are complaining about the free flow of drugs and the audacious daylight drug dealings happening on corners and alleys all around the neighborhood.

Now, my mother is rarely ever around, and honestly, I am not so bothered. The last time I saw her outside my school, she had offered to walk me home, but I had dance rehearsals and wanted to walk down to the community center. She had worn some sweatpants with these huge dark glasses. I knew there was something wrong with her. She did not talk much, though. Just asked how I was doing and how school was going. But when she knelt to give me a hug, I gently pulled down the sunglasses a little. It confirmed my greatest fear and every woman's worst nightmare; she was jumpy and seemed almost on the brink of tears. I did not ask her where or how she got the bruised eye, just pulled her into a hug and let her cry it out. I told her how much I loved her. My heart broke as I watched her adjust the dark sunglasses back into place and force a smile on her face. I wondered why she put herself through this type of pain. She told me not to tell my grandmother. I think she is ashamed because she did not come by the apartment for months after that afternoon.

Pum Pum Pum...

Again, I feel my heart beating fast and loud, bringing me back to the present. I almost reach out to cover my chest to prevent people from hearing it. I try to hide what is happening at home from my friends. Nelly, who is seated in the seat in front of me, turns her head back and winks at me. She is giddy and happy because Devon finally asked her to be his girlfriend after giving him some not-so-subtle hints over the past weeks. I am so happy classes are ending soon. I can go home and tell my grandma about the feels. She will definitely be able to put my mind at ease. I hope she is not sleeping. I don't want to wake her. Although, she has been sleeping a lot these days ...

Ggggrrnnnn!!!

The bell jerks me out of my thoughts. I distantly hear Mrs. Williams announce there will be a test next class, so I remind myself to make up for my distraction today by studying longer this evening. I like Geography, anyway.

Nelly puts her arms around me as we troop out of the class. Danielle also joins us, and we start chatting about who we think the new secret scribble in the girl's bathroom is about. Someone with funny handwriting usually writes secrets about girls and boys, always something about who is dating who. And the gist everyone is talking about is if Eva kissed Danny under the bleachers last week.

Danielle and Nelly have to stay after for Drama rehearsals. So, I walk back home alone. I like that because today, I really do feel like being alone with my thoughts. I decide to go through the park. I am so sure the scenery will make me feel better.

The day I asked my grandmother why they call autumn, fall season, she took me to the park and showed me the yellow and orange leaves that had fallen off the trees, creating a beautiful blanket of pretty leaves on the formerly dull ground.

"Baby, it's because this is the time when leaves fall."

"But why do they have to fall? Why can't they just stay in the trees and live forever?"

She shook her head and smiled at me. "We have to grow, honey. And if these leaves don't fall, new ones will not grow. I am sure in school they will teach you the science behind this process, but I want you to always remember that sometimes, even when it seems like bad things are happening, there is always a thing to be grateful for. Even when we don't want them to fall, they create beauty. Look at how beautiful the park is right now, and soon, when spring comes, there will be a new bloom. Just remember that, my love. There will always be a bloom. The worst will pass, and you will bloom again."

I walk through the park today, remembering what she said that day. I stand and stare at a tree, still struggling to let go of the bright orange leaves. I almost want to whisper to the tree that it is okay. That it will bloom again. But then again, I understand why this will be difficult. I cannot imagine what it is going through. I do not even like letting go. I mean, I have very little already; why do I have to give up more?

I continue to walk back home. I want to ask my grandmother more questions about the fall season.

When I approach my grandmother's building, I see my mother standing outside. A million things race through my mind. *Why is she here? Did she have a fight with my grandma? Is that why she is outside? Oh, I hope not. Things will get tense. Or worse, she may take me away from here. Maybe this is why I am feeling weird.*

As I move closer to her, she raises her head and finally sees me. But why does she have this look in her eyes like she is about to break? Not angry, not battered … kind of … sad.

What has happened? I am almost too scared to ask as I approach her.

There are some other people standing around her. Some faces I know, some I don't. I slow down until my legs feel too heavy to move. Something is wrong. I feel a chill in my bones … *Grandma? Is she sick? Will my mama have to move in to take care of her? Oh, I don't like the thought of that. Is my life about to change?*

Premonition spreads through my body as I slowly walk toward my mama again. She meets me halfway and pulls me into a hug.

"Oh, baby. I am so sorry. I am so … so sorry."

"Mama, what's wrong? Why are you crying? Please stop crying!"

She pulls back and looks at me. I see pity and pain in her eyes. Almost as if she is trying to prolong the inevitable.

"What's wrong?" I ask again. This time in a very faint trembling voice. Even though I am almost sure I really don't want to know. Something terrible has happened to someone … someone …

Then she says the word that gives me the fiercest pain I ever felt. "Your grandmother–"

"No," I whisper and step back, shaking my head as if I can stop her from making it real by saying the next words.

She put her hands to frame my face, trying to connect. "Honey, I am so sorry–

"NO!" This time, it is a scream as I run out of her grasp, past her, and into the building. Ignoring everyone who looks at me with such sad, pitiful eyes. I take the stairs as fast as my legs can carry me. My head and feet are numb to pain and exhaustion.

I open the door to find Pastor Harris and some other women from the church. I escape as Mrs. Richardson, the choir leader, tries to pull me in for a hug. I immediately run past them and into my grandmother's bedroom. Expecting to find her taking her nap. But it is empty.

There is something missing. I look around, locking every piece of accessories and furniture into my mind. Analyzing, assessing, looking for something.

Looking for life ... because that is what is missing. *Life*.

The person I love the most in the world is gone. I get so overwhelmed by sadness and pain that it literally takes my breath away, and I struggle to breathe. I can only let out short pants as tears well in my eyes. I let out a loud wail of loss. I continue to cry heavy body-rocking tears that blind my eyes with tears and shoot pain through my head.

I grab her old quilt off her bed as I sniff in her scent. I wrap it around my body and roll into the smallest ball on the ground. And with every second, it sinks into my mind that I will never see my grandma again, or hear her deep, robust laughter, watch her bend over her stove, listen to her stories, or her answers to my ridiculous questions. Right here and now, I know exactly how it feels to literally have your heart broken into a thousand pieces and know there is no way you can feel whole again because a huge part of your heart is lost forever. *Gone*.

Just like the person I love the most in the world.

Chapter Three
Different Boats: 2009

"CAN'T BELIEVE WE ARE going to college," Nelly says as she digs in the bucket for another chicken wing.

"Bitch, speak for yourself," Danielle says. "I can't believe we are ADULTS now. Like, is it just me? I don't feel smarter than I was last year just because I am already eighteen. Can't believe my folks want me to start paying rent this year." Danielle rolls her eyes as she also reaches into the bucket.

We are at Danielle's folk's place, having our own version of a graduation party. We got some balloons from the dollar store to fill the popcorn ceiling in the dining room. Danielle's parents have mint green couches in the living room. We aren't allowed to sit on them, so we're partying in the dining room with the gold antique table and chairs. Nelly's family will be putting something together another day to celebrate us getting into college. I am going to Eastern Michigan University, a public research university in Ypsilanti, while Nelly is going to The University of Michigan, Ann Arbor, which is just a short drive away from Ypsilanti. Both Nelly and I got into our choice schools. Even though I am lucky enough to have gotten a partial scholarship and student loans, I still have to work during all my free hours to make up for it. Danielle is choosing not to go to college so she can put more work and time into her singing career.

Danielle had made some fried chicken and mac and cheese and invited us over since her parents are out of town and Nelly's folks are driving her crazy with suggestions on what she should major in, oblivious to the fact that she is going through an identity phase right now. I guess Danielle and I are the only ones that know this. Since she was ten, she has wanted to be a doctor. Now she doesn't know if she wants to be a doctor or if everyone else wants her to be a doctor, like her stepfather, who she adores so much. Danielle, on the other hand, does know what she wants to do and will spend her time recording some songs to try and get a record deal in New York. This decision is driving her parents crazy because nothing they had said—or done—has changed her mind. In fact, she has been saving to move out to New York for more than a year now.

For me, however, the past few years have not been peachy. I have been so focused on getting into a good college that I never took the time to consider what I would do when I get there. I don't know what I want yet, but it definitely has to be something of service to people. My focus on getting into college also had me falling behind in other aspects of my life. To the point where I feel pathetic.

We wolf down food as we discuss our paths.

"It is almost depressing that the last boyfriend I had was in middle school. What was I doing during high school?! I never even looked at any guys!" I say.

Danielle chuckles mischievously. "Whoa! Okay. Guess we are doing this today then," she comments with her mouth still full as she chews fast enough to make her point. "I will tell you what you were doing. You were busy slaving away at every job you could find." She is not wrong but hearing it from her kinda hits a nerve. I feel hurt that this is how my friend thinks of me. Even though she is not being intentionally ignorant, it's obvious that our reality is different. I always felt like what I was doing was right and, honestly, my only option. Even though her parents may not be mega-rich, Danielle's father is a landscaper, and her mother is a nurse. They always supported her dreams and took care of her every need. The only odd jobs she ever did were whenever she wanted spending money. And Nelly's stepfather is a darling who is ready to give her anything she wants. I don't resent them for their lives. But for someone like me, my only choice is to work for the future I want.

I could call her out for her being insensitive, but that's just going to end up being a whole thing. Instead, I roll my eyes and shrug my response.

"Getting into college has always felt like my only chance if I don't want to end up like my mother. Plus, I promised my grandma I would do everything I could to make something of myself."

"Do you even know what that is?" Nelly asks.

"What do you mean?" I return, taken by her question.

"You say you promised your grandmother that you would make something of yourself, and you have saved so much over the last four years and have studied so hard. What exactly do you want to make of yourself?"

"Oh—I—uhh …"

I am honestly speechless. All through high school, I kept waiting for something to hit me. Like my grandmother always felt the need to take care of people and ended up being a nurse.

What do I want to make of myself? The simple answer is that I don't know. My future has never had a face. Like me seeing myself as a lawyer in a courthouse or as a doctor in a hospital. I just always wanted to feel … safe and financially secure. All shades of different from what I grew up with my mother. Definitely not a situation where I can ever be abused by someone like Sean.

I do feel like the pressure to do better has made me want to do better. I have been chasing money for so long, I haven't even let myself stop and think about what I want to do for the rest of my life.

"You have never said exactly what you want to major in. Have you ever thought about it?" Nelly presses again.

"I don't know. Is that not what college is for?" I say, trying to get her off my back.

Danielle interjects after taking a sip of her soda. "Yeah, but as *Black women*, we don't have the time for that white-people-confused-phase shit."

Nelly raises her brows. "I think we hold Black women to too much of a high standard. If she needs time to figure it out, then I think she should take her time."

"This is not about that. You know Crystal. She sets her mind on something and goes for it. I am just worried she is not going to college with a big picture in mind. She does not have anything to go on." Danielle explains her point to Nelly to calm her down before she takes things personally.

Now I really do not like this back and forth about my life. Especially when it is about MY life and future. Something they have no idea about. I know they mean well, but they are starting to project their anxieties into my life, and I really have to put a stop to it.

I sit up and raise my hand to signal a time-out.

"Hello?!" I wave my hands. "I am right here! You can stop the commentary about me like I am not in the room." I turn my head to the right. "Point taken, Nelly." And to the left. "And I don't need this kind of pressure, Danielle." I exhale, raise my hands in a shrug and smile cheekily. "Look, I got into college, Bitches! Let's eat some chicken and celebrate, please!"

"Fine! Backing off, Crystal." Nelly rolls her eyes and raises her hand in surrender. "Retracting the claws," she adds in the tone of a fake banshee.

We burst into hearty laughter that fills the room.

"At least *you* have a direction, Crystal," Nelly says with her eyes gleaming in mischief. She is trying to pull Danielle's leg.

"Bitch, please. Don't tell me you are in my house, eating my food, and giving me attitude? Really?" Danielle bites back. Clearly, she is in no mood for Nelly's passive-aggressive attitude today.

"What! No. I am just concerned for you, that's all. Just checking to be sure you know what you are doing. New York is not Detroit, you know?" Nelly returns, trying to absolve herself and her intentions.

"You don't say." Danielle rolls her eyes. "Don't you think I know that?!" Danielle rolls her eyes again as she rushes for a napkin to clean her hands and dab her shirt to clean out the tiny drop of ketchup on it. Danielle continues, "Look, I know New York is hard, and that is kind of why I want to go there. To prove to myself, to my folks, and you guys that I know what I am doing. Y'all know I got the voice."

I decide to interrupt before Nelly says something that makes it worse. "Everyone in this town knows what raw talent you are packing in that pretty throat," I say to Danielle. A compliment that earns me a smile and promises a safe landing for what I want to say next. "It's just that, it is New York. We have heard stories of people going there with dreams and getting lost in the city with nothing to show for it.

You are a Black woman in America with a big voice, no doubt—but have you really considered all your options? Are you sure this is what you want to do right now, Danielle?"

Danielle sighs and gives me a sweet smile. "First of all, I love you." She turns to Nelly. "And I love you, too." She then shrugs. "We have had several variations of this conversation for about a year now since I told you guys of my plans to go to New York. Look, I know it is scary. Especially for me. But hey, we got ourselves a fine-ass Black President! Who would have ever thought that was possible? Ladies, we are in the prime of our lives when we can take risks and either learn from them or make something out of them. You don't know what college is going to be like when you get there, but you are going anyway." She points at Nelly. "You want to be a doctor; I say go for it. But don't limit your mind. Make new friends, have new experiences. And Crystal, for God's sake, ditch work and have some fun! Take a damn break for once in your life and breathe. Give yourself the grace to figure life out and what makes you happy and giddy without expectations."

Danielle takes a deep breath. "I know I don't have it all figured out yet. But I will. I will go to New York and chase my dreams. I will give myself a chance. If it doesn't work out, then fine. But I will try. Girls, you know we are hustlers. And I have come this far. It's time to break out of the safety net of Detroit and get out into the world. I am ready."

Now there are tears in my eyes, listening to my friend speak with such conviction. Among the three of us, it's so surprising to see that she seems to have it together. Danielle has never been one for school, so college was out of the question. A fact that frustrated her parents. In our neighborhood, everyone assumes the best way to make it out is through a successful career, and you get that in college. So, Danielle saying she is not going to college is like saying she is not ready to aim high or make something out of herself. And she has had to fight that negativity from people for a while now. Even though sometimes doubt pries its way into her mind. So listening to her speak this way makes me proud of how far she has come in her journey of self-discovery.

"You never know unless you try, right?" I say to Danielle before I stand up to give her a hug. "I am so proud of you."

Nelly joins in. "And we will be rooting for you."

We stay like that for minutes. Enjoying the moment. Knowing that our entire lives are about to change and that we are each taking different boats on uncharted waters. But I am very confident that I am always going to have these ladies in my corner. My own tribe.

"Okay, okay, okay." Danielle breaks out of the hug and quickly wipes the tears that have pooled in her eyes. "Enough of all this mushiness. Let's dance!"

"Yes!" We chorus as Danielle rushes to the sound system to put in a CD.

"Check out this mix Christian made for me when he heard I was moving to New York." Danielle turns to us, beaming as she waves a CD in our faces.

"Aww, Christian, your white boy lab partner that always had an eye for you and worships the ground you walk on?" Nelly teases and lunges to try and grab it from her, but Danielle is quick.

"That boy has been in love with you since we were ten. Are you taking him with you to New York? I am pretty sure he's gonna be down for that ride." I suggest to Danielle while winking and wriggling my brow.

"Shut up, Crystal. Of course, he is not." Danielle chuckles. "Not taking any baggage with me to New York," Danielle's eyes dart to Nelly, "unlike some people I know."

Nelly takes the bait and starts defending herself. "I don't know the problem y'all have with me and Noah dating and going to college together. We 'bout to Michelle and Barack y'all in the next few years."

"Babe, we both know Noah is no way close to being a Barack. That dude may be book smart, but he definitely is not street smart. And Barack ... is both." Danielle clarifies.

"You mean the Ivy-league Barack Obama?" I join in the act just to tease Nelly.

"You mean fine-ass, chocolate-dripping, sweet-like-rum Barack." Leave it to Danielle to have a crush on a man old enough to be her father.

I better interject because she can go about how she loves an older black man with a sprinkle of silver hair.

"Okay! Enough. This has gone to a weird place. Nelly, as long as you are happy going to the University of Michigan with Noah, you do you, girl. Just don't lose yourself in that relationship."

"I won't, thank you very much, *Friend*." Nelly intentionally stresses the last word. Even though she was responding to me, she sticks her tongue out to Danielle. "Suck it, Danielle."

"As long as it's not Noah's dick."

We burst out laughing, remembering the time Nelly told us about Noah crying one time after she gave him a blowjob. We had just started out as freshmen in high school we were introduced to the sex-craze of high school kids. So Nelly had suggested they have sex for the first time. To ease into it, she said she would give a blowjob first. Both fifteen years old, both amateurs. One afternoon when his parents were out, they decided to do the dirty, only for Noah to scream so loud when he came that Nelly almost ran out of there. It was when he was zipping his pants that she discovered he had tears in his eyes. And he had loved it so much that he cried his release. We laughed so hard when she told us; I am so sure she wished she never did. Although, I am surprised they never hound me for being a virgin. Danielle has had a ton of boyfriends, and even with just Noah, Nelly has had some sexual adventure as well. I never told anyone, but a part of me is happy that Justin moved away before we got past the stage of holding hands and light pecks on the cheeks. Ever since that incident with Sean, I still cannot imagine being naked in front of any man. Just the thought alone takes me back to the morning I was helpless under his gaze. And every guy I try to date, when I know it might get serious, I break it off and just use work as an excuse. No one knows what happened with Sean, but I suspect Nelly and Danielle know something is up with my avoiding relationships. I suspect they think my mother's terrible choices are what traumatized me. I am grateful they chose not to push the issue all these years. Well, until today.

Danielle finally plays a song that gets us grooving as soon as the sound comes on. A smile spread on my face as we lip-sync to Janet Jackson's *All for You.*

This is our jam. More like our song. The three of us (we practically forced Danielle, but she eventually loved it) even did a song-dance performance during a talent show competition in middle school. We did not win, but we had so much fun, and since then, it has become our song.

I jump on my feet and pull Nelly up to join us. We dance around the living room, bopping to Janet's feisty energy, letting ourselves feel young and happy.

I will miss this. This time with my favorite people that I feel closer to than my mother. We may live in the same house, but we are more like roommates, co-existing in the same space with as little contact as possible. Only talking to each other when we have to. I go to school and go to work. Intentionally trying to stay away from meeting any of the men she brings home. There have even been times when I never meet the men. I just know when they break up because my mother retreats into her room for days, and the house becomes filthy and disheveled. When that happens, I come home to fix dinner and clean the house. But soon, she bounces back and starts seeing someone new again, and I go back to leaving notes for her on the refrigerator.

There was one person, though, a few years ago. Just one time, I let myself hope that it would work out with–

GRNNNN!! GRRNNNN!!!

My phone alarm rings and breaks into my thoughts as I stop dancing and start frantically searching for my phone.

"Oh shit!"

"What's up?" Nelly asks with raised brows at the alarm in my voice and my use of expletives.

"I really should be at work in about ten minutes, or Ricky is going to take half of my paycheck," I answer.

Danielle rolls her eyes in obvious frustration like she has done for the past four years every time I have had to go to work. "I don't think Ricky will be mad if you take a day off, which you should have done."

"Well, I cannot leave them hanging. And I need the money if I am going to be able to afford my own place when I move to Ypsilanti. Can't be staying in those dusty ass dorms," I say to Danielle as I look around for my purse, speaking slowly and not letting my frustration show because I know they mean well.

"I don't think it will be that bad. Really," Danielle interjects with a twinkle in her eye. "You could meet new friends, forget about us. Y'all would go wild together and become a Ypsi hippie."

I chuckle. "No way. I don't want dem people all up in my business. Guess I am stuck with you guys until we all check into some old folk's facility to reign hell there when we are old and gross."

I find my purse on the edge of the sofa and grab it while wiggling back into my loafers as I try to reach for another piece of chicken for the road.

"I do worry about you, Crys," Nelly says as she watches me through her mother-hen gaze. "You have been breaking your back before it was legal for you to hold down a job. You probably would not have a social life if not for us dragging you out every now and then. I just hope you don't continue at this pace in college."

I nod while listening, my mouth half-open as I throw a wink and manage a smile at Danielle's cocked head; worry is evident on her face as well.

I shrug and bite down on my piece of wings. "Look, guys. I can't promise anything, but I will try to have a semblance of a life."

"It also would not hurt to start saying yes to things. Like dates?" Nelly shrugs while intentionally avoiding my face but excessively blinks to prove a point.

"I have said yes to dates." I try to defend myself. "I have even dated a lot of guys."

"Oh please, none of those dates lived to become a real relationship or someone you can call a boyfriend." Nelly calls me out and quickly adds, "Middle school boyfriends don't even count."

"Yep. Justin moved before we even got to high school, and you know middle school boyfriends are not official," says Danielle.

Nelly rolls her eyes. "Not that he was much of a prize either, just saying."

Danielle follows with a chuckle. "Remember those buck teeth, and he had that weird one-sided afro?"

I quickly swoop in to save the poor boy from being devoured by my friends. "Come on, guys. He was fourteen. He was growing. And he was nice." I try to defend my first love.

"Yeah, yeah, our point is that it is not normal to have your first and only relationship when you are fourteen. Get out there and sow some wild oats, gal!" Danielle comments with her hand pointing outside.

I sigh and chuckle. "He did have those huge buck teeth."

"Yep!" They chorus to my admission.

"And you know what? It is time for some yes-es." I continue.

"You go, Crystal!" Nelly hyped in her super pumped pitchy voice. She then goes on to say, "In fact, this summer before college, you should start saying some more yes-es. Just to practice."

I roll my eyes in surrender and groan in defeat. "Fine, I will. Now, I really have to go."

I grab both of them into a bear hug. A type we have shared millions of times over the years. My girls … ride or die. It's weird how I am not afraid that we will fall out. For people like us, we are more sisters than friends. I am more worried about the future and my new life ahead.

We pull back, and I pick up some paper towels to clean my hands as I dash out of the house.

I finish the last of the chicken in my mouth and balance my purse over my shoulder as I start to clean my fingers, walking at a brisk pace to make my shift at the Ricky's Pizza Plaza, which is more of a small restaurant. But it is kid-friendly, which makes it a favorite in the neighborhood. Although, kid-friendly does mean more work for the staff who has to cater to loud, whiny children. The tip usually makes up for the stress. I have been working there for over three years now, and I will be leaving for college in six weeks. Ricky's way of showing how much love he has for me is to be harder on me during my last few weeks. Giving me longer hours and calling me up for every shift someone calls in sick for. I am not even mad at it. Ricky is a fair but strict boss, and I will miss working there. He even lets me pick up extra shifts most weekends. In his own way, he is trying to help me make more money before I have to leave for college.

My phone beeps again, and I reach for it without stopping. With my head bent, I don't see the person coming, and as I finally get to my phone, I feel a warm body slam against mine. And then I hear a familiar voice, one I never would have thought I would hear again.

"Oh my God!" I hear someone exclaim. "Crystal!?"

I shake my head and cock it to the side with a sly grin as I confirm my suspicion about who it is.

"Justin?! Wow."

"Crystal!"

He looks almost unrecognizable now. Gone are the buck teeth and weird hairstyle. He is now muscular and lean, like a swimmer, and his teeth are all white and perfect. He has short locks that fall around his dark chiseled face and makes the light bounce off his handsome face. No one would believe this is the same awkward teenager from four years ago.

He looks confident in his jeans and oversize blue sweater. And he is rocking Nike Air Max Lebron VII—good, Lord! I know my sneakers, and his kicks are HOT right now. I do not ogle men, but I almost cannot believe how attractive Justin is looking right now.

"You look really good!" I blurt. My eyes bulge as if they

want to pop out of my socket, and I am sure my face would be the darkest shade of red right now if I was white. I, for sure, thought he would run away when I gave the compliment but instead, he looks like he is blushing.

Wait, is he really flattered?

He gives me a sweet smile as he looks over at me and nods with an appreciative smile.

"Wow. You—girl, you look fantastic. How does it seem like your face has just manifested into a surreal beauty that resembles a goddess?!"

His words make me feel all warm and fuzzy inside. I don't know when I start smiling, but I have to look away from him for a few seconds.

"Good to know you are still so good with words," I say with a nod of acknowledgment. Of course, he has to have seen what those words did to me. Even I am surprised; no one has ever made me feel this way. Well, no one has ever said the things Justin said, the way he said it. I clear my throat, "So, ermm.. do you still write poems?"

"Oh, you mean those poems I used to write for you about you?" He raises his brows and slightly narrows his eyes as he shoots me a timid smile.

I almost don't recognize myself when my body gets hot all over. I turn my head away, trying and failing to hide my smile while I nod. This gorgeous guy is making me sweat from the middle of my back down to my butt. This is very surprising, even for me. I have not let myself feel this way about any guy since that incident with Sean years ago. Mainly because I know most teenage boys are hormone-crazed and only want to get inside your pants. Not that I am against sex in general, I just usually want to crawl out of my skin or immediately want to take a shower when I think about a guy seeing me naked.

But for the first time, I feel something different. I almost want to reach out and trace the line of his well-trimmed beard and stroke his pretty face down to those lips–

"So still a poet, huh? Everyone thought you were really good." I yank myself out of those dangerous thoughts with a quick headshake.

"Oh, wait. You mean your friends thought so? When they would read my letters to you and laugh?!"

I chuckle with guilt. "No. I mean, yes. But not just them. Remember when you wrote the poem about Black Independence that had everyone clapping? Even Mrs. Brenda said you have a really good head on your shoulders."

He nods. "I remember those words of high praise from the stone-faced Mrs. Brenda." He closes his eyes and dramatically clutches his chest. "They shaped my life."

We burst out laughing at the epic day when the strictest teacher gave him a compliment. The first and last I ever heard her give anyone.

"It's a shame you moved away. You might have been lucky to score another compliment out of her."

"Nah, I don't think so. It was just the smart thing to do, to leave while the ovation was the loudest."

I roll my eyes and snicker at his humor.

"But for real though," I continue. "You just left all of a sudden. Right in the middle of the school year. And we never heard from you again."

Actually, I want to say "*I*" never heard from him again, but it's better I play it safe. He probably doesn't even remember us dating for those few weeks before he left. We were fourteen. It was just for the summer. Sometimes, I think I read more into it than it ever was. Not that we were ever really official boyfriend and girlfriend or anything like that. We just hung out a lot and stared into each other's eyes. Maybe he even did that with a ton of other girls back then.

"Yeah, I am so sorry about that. It took me by surprise too. My dad had gotten a job out of town and just wanted us to leave right away. But not long after that, he got fired for drinking on the job and did not want to come back here in shame, so he moved us to New Orleans. We lost my mom a few months after that, and in the middle of that roller coaster, I tried to reach you, but it was so difficult–"

"Hey, I understand." Honestly, I don't know if I do. I feel conflicted. This is all taking me by surprise. The fact he had just left suddenly without a goodbye or a phone call all these years. I just assumed he moved on and forgot about me. And now to find out that he has also been through a lot …

"No. I owe you an explanation–"

"Look. Really, I get it. We were young. You were going through a lot, and we just drifted apart. It happens."

"I just want you to know that I made an effort. That you were worth the effort."

I give a little shrug and quirk a part of my mouth to hide a happy smile. "Anyway. It's great to see you even though it's been four years. What are you doing in town anyway?"

"Well, I'm writing my novel, and it's kinda set in this city. Just graduated high school a few weeks back, and I'm on tour right now with a band I joined in New Orleans. I have been looking forward to coming back for the past years. There was no doubt in my mind that I had to see you again. And here I was thinking about how to make that possible when you almost knocked me over in the street."

I scoff in funny exasperation. "No way! *You* almost knocked *me* down. I am the victim."

He raises his hand in surrender. "Okay, okay. Geez! You can have this one."

"And what are the chances that I meet you here? Just coming from my hangout with Nelly and Danielle, and you came up–"

"Wow. Really flattering to know I am still a subject of conversation amongst you three, even years later."

"Shut up. We were just talking about me still being single and putting myself out there more." I almost put my hands over my mouth and sink into the ground as I realize the admission I just made to Justin. He must think I am trying to flirt or give him a nudge to ask me out. To be honest, I really want him to.

"Oh." He gives a wide smile now; his eyes gleam with excitement. "Okay, Crystal. That is great to know."

Shit! I quickly glance at my phone, gasp to salvage my pride, and find a place to knock my head on a wall for being so stupid and loose-mouthed.

"I am sorry, I have to go, Justin. Really running late for work. But it was great seeing you, and maybe we can catch up sometime." I actually said the last part out of courtesy.

"How about we catch up today? Where do you work? I can walk with you while we talk details about high school in Detroit and New Orleans, particularly why all the guys in this city are so blind and dense to leave a gorgeous gal single." A warm bliss of happiness spreads to my body when he said this before I could walk past him.

I am flattered but still will not give him the satisfaction of knowing that.

"No one *left* me single. I just have not had time to date. I work at Ricky's. It's just around the corner if you want to walk with me."

He flashes me his wide teeth, and I can almost feel his joy when I tell him he can walk me to work. Like a kid that has been given an unlimited pass to the rollercoaster. He falls into step beside me as he tells me about his life in New Orleans.

He lived there with his dad, who had just recently met a woman, and they are talking about getting married. Justin is not too crazy about the woman, but he is happy his father is doing well and good enough that he could leave because half of his job had been making sure his dad was not nose-deep in the bottom of the bottle. He seems to also enjoy playing with the band. He plays the guitar and piano. I knew he could play the piano even while he was here, but he must have picked up guitar along the way too. He does not plan to go to college. He doesn't see a need for it. He already knows what he wants to be. A Nobel prize winner—in literature. He wants to write his novel. The first of many legendary reads, he promises. No, I cannot read what he has written yet—I asked. He just got into town a week ago and is staying at the motel with the rest of the band while he convinces them to stay in Detroit for the rest of the summer so he can write his book. He just needs to secure residency of some sort in a big club downtown. He loves New Orleans, and he actually developed his love for music there. He is single and wants to see me tomorrow night.

That last part seems to go over my head. He says something, but I just stare there, and it takes a moment for my brain to register that he had asked a question even as we stand in front of the side door to Ricky's. I am very late, but I don't care. I am standing in front of the boy of my dreams; everything else can wait.

"Wait. Are you asking me out on a date?"

"Yes. This is cosmic fate. I finally see the girl I have been dreaming about for the last four years. I don't want to waste another minute. Please say yes, Crystal."

"Ummmm …" I want to tell him that I have not gone on a

date before. That I don't know what to do or say when on a date. We have only ever hung out in public ... and that was four years ago! We are basically two different *adults* now. And I have no experience to bring to the table. Not that I ever intend to let him know that.

"Look, it's going to be very simple, I promise. Just the two of us hanging out, catching up. Just like we have been doing this afternoon."

"Okay." That is as much as I can bring myself to squeak out.

"Okay?" he repeats as a sweet smile slowly spreads across his glistening ebony face.

"Okay. Let's do it," I added this time.

He nods vigorously, unable to hide his enthusiasm. "That's great. Let's say 5 p.m. We will go catch a movie and then grab something to eat."

"That sounds good. Let me give you my number."

"Yes. Please do." He pulls out his iPhone 3G. I dial my number in and hand it over to him to save it however he wants. I heard guys like to save with ridiculous IDs. Who knows what he will save mine as. Guess we will have to wait and see.

We finally say goodbye, and I walk over to the side door that the staff and delivery guys use to access the restaurant. I walk in with caution, fully expecting Ricky to read me the riot act, which, in my opinion, is totally worth it for the wonderful past few minutes I just had with Justin.

Lucky for me, it seems Ricky is also running late, and Mario, the supervisor and head cook, is out running errands, so there is no one else to scold me for coming late. I am pretty sure the rest of the guys will definitely cover for me. We look out for each other like that.

I grab my uniform, change my loafers to my comfortable

work sneakers, then say hello to my colleagues as we quickly exchange pleasantries and quick gossip.

I go about taking orders and bringing out food to the customers, but my mind is in a million other places.

My phone rings again, and this time, I wince and let out a silent curse when I pull out my phone to see the person calling. It is Deja. Deja is one of my closest friends. She is practically my sister, I mean, it's a long story how that came to be, but ever since we were twelve, we have claimed ourselves to be family. Not by blood but by love.

This is the third time she is calling, as I have missed her other calls earlier today. Once while I was with the girls and the other when I was with Justin.

I make a signal to my colleague, Rose, at the other end of the restaurant, that I am going to take a quick bathroom break. So, I let the phone ring as I make my way through the kitchen to the tiny but clean staff bathroom and changing room. The best place to catch a break if you don't want to leave the building.

And it's really great Deja is calling. She gives the best guy advice anyway, and she is always so on point fashion-wise; it makes you feel like she has her whole life all figured out. Even though she, of course, plans to have her own fashion line and become a stylist to the stars, she is currently working in a boutique but hopes to save enough to move to LA next year to, like she would say it, embrace her destiny!

She is a drama queen. Total opposite of me. Which is probably why we hit it off since we were twelve and have always seen ourselves as sisters even though our parents' relationship fizzled out a long time ago. My mom had met her dad when I was twelve, and I had promised myself not to care about anyone she dated. Indifference was my superpower back then. But after dating for a few months, they decided it was time for the children to meet. On a lucky Saturday afternoon, Deja and her brother Tyler were dragged to the amusement park to meet their divorced father's new girlfriend's daughter—me.

They must have come with the same mind I did because after they not-so-subtly left us alone to hang, it got pretty exhausting keeping the frown, so I complimented Tyler on his kicks. Turns out he is a sneakerhead like me. And they both love Harry Potter. Not a lot of my friends did back then.

And that was how we became close friends. Almost inseparable, really. Even though we went to different schools, we always kept in touch and hung out as much as we could. Not even our parents breaking up a few months later could break the bond between me and Deja. And Rachel. Rachel is Deja's cousin. They more or less live together since Rachel's mom is a single parent and travels a lot for work, so Rachel ends up staying with Deja and Tyler a lot.

Surprisingly, Rachel is more my spirit animal, kind of like an old soul. And while I love Deja dearly, I find myself closer to Rachel. She is the one I can tell anything to and be sure she will understand and not judge me. In fact, she is the only one I have ever tried to tell about what happened with Sean. I struggled to put it into words, but she just let me cry it out on her shoulder. After that day, she never asked again, and I never offered to talk about it. But with a little hand squeeze or sometimes a simple nod, she acknowledges my struggles. She is the only one on the planet that I feel can relate to me completely. I love Deja, Nelly, and Danielle, but sometimes I feel they have no real clue. But Rachel gets it. Maybe because we both grew up with absent mothers and disappeared fathers, we are able to connect on so many deep levels.

I locate an empty stall in the bathroom and enter. I lock

the door as I sit on the closed toilet seat before dialing Deja's number.

Her high-pitched, super excited, always breezy voice picks up on the second ring. "Hey, sis!"

"Hi, babe. I am so sorry I missed your call. It's been a crazy day. I will tell you all about it later."

"No worries. You know, Rachel is here in the store, and we are thinking about dropping by. When is your break coming up?"

I check my watch. "Actually. I just got here about an hour ago. But you guys can drop by when my shift is over. We will catch up then. I've got something to tell you."

"Oh great! Now you've got me anticipating this. We will drive through when I close the shop."

No sooner had I said my goodbyes did my phone vibrate to signify an incoming text message.

"I still cannot believe my luck that I finally found you today ... by bumping into you on the street! Anyway, I am still struggling to believe it. Can you say something to convince me that I spoke to the girl of my dreams this afternoon?"

"I have to say, this is a nice upgrade from the lovesick puppy notes you used to sneak into my backpack in middle school!"

"What? Lol. I am so sorry I had no game back then. I promise I am better now."

"Better now, huh? I guess you will have to prove that to me then."

"Oh, it will be my pleasure. So we start tomorrow. Get ready, babe!"

"I thought you said it would be us hanging out. Like, say movies and some fries was the plan?!

"Oh, it is. It is ... but I do have some surprises up my sleeves. Just get ready."

"Great! Look forward to it!"

A small giggle escapes my lips, and I put my hands over my mouth, trying to shake my head of all the girly emotions swimming through the belly. I quickly text him back that I have to return to work, and he lets me know that we will talk later.

I am new to this feeling. I am probably late to it, but I am pretty new to feeling this way about any guy, especially one I just met. I mean, he is no stranger, really. Or maybe that is part of the charm.

I take another look at our whole text exchange, biting my upper lip. Maybe I will ask Deja for some tips on flirting. She is pretty good at it. She has been able to charm and flirt her way out of anything since she was fifteen. Not only is she the coolest, but she is also absolutely gorgeous with her Pocahontas features, and she knows it too.

After about five minutes of daydreaming about how the date will go tomorrow, I finally snap out of it and step out of the bathroom stall to splash some water on my face. It has a way of helping me get back to the present. Right now, I have a job to do, and I had better go back outside and get that job done.

I work almost on autopilot now. Been doing this for so

long that I know the entire menu in my head and know when to smile and nod and do all the right things a waitress should do.

Time flies by, and Liya, another waitress, walks up to me. "Ricky said to tell you your shift is over, and you should go home and rest."

"Thanks, Liya."

My phone rings, and I smile when I see Deja's name on the tiny screen.

"Hey, right on time. My shift just ended."

"Great! We are pulling up now."

I stretch my legs to look outside and roll my eyes. "No, you're not. I am looking out right now."

"Well, we are pretty close."

"Pretty close is not the same thing as being in front." I head to the back of the restaurant to change out of my work shirt and grab my bag, chuckling as she tries to wiggle her way out of being caught in a lie. I am so sure she has on her classic pouting face.

"You know that parking is hell on your block, and we are in a hurry. So you better have your ass out of your restaurant, or I swear to God, I will go on a date with Ricky and become your boss, and guess what, I will have you wearing the tiniest shorts. Shorter than Hooters and doing the stanky dance on every table that tips you–"

"That is scary as fuck, Deja!" I burst out laughing as I make my way out the staff exit door on the side of the restaurant. "And shut up. I can see you guys," I say into the phone as I wave my hands at the approaching car. Rachel is driving, and Deja is in the passenger seat with her phone to her ear. I quickly remember we are still on a call. I quickly yell, "Bye!"

The car comes to a stop beside me, and Deja pushes her

head out and greets me with a huge smile on her face. Undoubtedly one of the sweetest and happiest people I have ever met. Since the first day we met, she has wormed her way into my life with her infectious happy spirit. You really can not help but love Deja. She is one of my favorite people. And stunningly beautiful. Her brown skin glows in the sun. Her oval-shaped face houses features that will make a painter jump on a canvas. And did I mention that she has the best sense of style? Her dream is actually to be a stylist and fashion designer. She has been making and choosing outfits for me and Rachel since we were in middle school. She currently works in a fancy boutique where she spreads her charm to make huge sales. To be honest, it is almost impossible to not fall for her charm. Her energy is infectious. She makes you want to smile without even knowing why.

"Hiii!" Deja screams as she pulls her top half through the passenger side window.

"Hi," I respond as I walk toward the car. "Hey, Rachy."

Rachel is like the opposite of Deja, while I am a mixture of both of their personalities. Deja is an extrovert that derives joy from being around people. Rachel would rather do the opposite. Yet, they get along so well because Rachel has spent most of her life living with Deja.

"So, this is you guys just pulling up five minutes ago, huh?" I accuse them, raising their eyebrows and making a terrible attempt to fake an angry face.

"That's all, Deja," Rachel says as she folds her arms together and rests on the car door where the windows have been rolled down.

Deja just laughs and says, "Well, I did say, 'Pretty close.'"

"How–"

"Just get in! We might get a ticket, and you know we are

too broke as a group to afford one," she says and returns back into her seat as she opens the back door from inside for me.

"Well, I am sure you will just dust off your good ol' charm and get us out of it," I tease as I step into the back of the car.

Rachel and I burst out laughing as we looked at Deja's frown. She shoots us daggers with an intense stare that makes us laugh even harder.

"I will have you know, ladies, that there is more to it than batting eyelashes. It's less flirting and more reading people. When I see a person, I instantly have an idea of who they are and how best to interact with them. That's how I sell clothes and accessories. If you play nice, I can teach you."

"Oh, how come you don't use this God-Given skill to make your relationship with Aaron work? I mean, you guys have been on and off again for the past three years; no one can keep up," Rachel pipes in as she pulls out into the road.

"It is true. *Madam interactor*, how come you're not *interacting* a breakup with Aaron when that is what you really want instead of taking him back again and again out of pity," I ask.

"That is different. And you know it. Me and Aaron have got some Bonnie and Clyde thing going on," Deja responds.

"Oh please, Bonnie and Clyde, my ass. You just get lost in those puppy brown eyes and lose all your critically acclaimed guts. You are too nice for your own good," Rachel pitches in.

"It doesn't matter anyway. He is going to Harvard on a full-ride, and I am going to leave our imminent breakup to distance. Distance, they say, causes the college heart to forget you," she says, very proud of herself and the metaphor she definitely just made up.

I roll my eyes. Deja can be delusional sometimes. "While

keeping the door open as the sweet ex that never broke his heart. If you think that guy will ever let you go, you've got something else coming."

"Oh, you wait and see. I've got a plan." Deja winks before turning back to face me. "Okay, spill. What do you have to tell us?"

"So, have I ever told you guys about Justin?" I am giddy with excitement and dart my eyes from Deja to Rachel, almost squealing to blurt out my news.

"Justin? Have you told us about Justin? Is he not the same guy you could not shut up about back in middle school?" Deja answers with her brow raised in curiosity.

"How could we ever forget your one and only *boyfriend*. You were the first of us to have one. We were so jealous of you, and you could not stop gushing about his letters … or were they poems?"

"No, he was not a boyfriend," Deja corrects using air quotes. "But there were poems," Deja chips in to clarify. "She used to read it aloud without understanding a thing he wrote," Deja jokes.

"It's really difficult for me to understand complicated poems. There is a name for the condition, you know?"

"Yeah, right," says Deja.

"So, why are we talking about him, Crystal?" Rachel asks. She must have sensed a story brewing as she swerved through the streets of Detroit.

"Wait, where are we going?" I ask.

"To the Roostertail. My boss is having a birthday party–" Deja says.

"Has she not already had one this year?" I interrupt.

"Oh, that was the official one, but this is the one she chose for herself. Honestly, it's just a chance to drink booze and act crazy with her friends. I think they rented out the entire place, so it is free food. We are just going to dash in and out. Score some food and drinks and head over to the waterfront," Deja explains.

Deja and her boss, Shemiah, who likes to believe she is twenty-five even though she really is thirty-one, have an odd and complicated relationship. I think she is just one of those people that never grows up. It's like Shemiah loves Deja and is jealous of her at the same time. So, Deja is never able to predict her reaction to things which is why she probably wants to make an appearance at this party just in case. Because while Shemiah pays Deja well, not caring that she is a teenager, she does not hesitate to play the role of the classic boss-bitch most times.

"Okay then. At least, we will get some free food out of this."

"You were saying something about Justin. Go on, sis," Deja says.

"Yeah, Justin. You guys will not believe this. Earlier this morning, I was with Nelly and Danielle because Danielle will be leaving soon for New York in a few weeks–"

"Oh my God. That's amazing. I am so happy she is finally doing it. So, so proud," Deja interjects as she beams from ear to ear. She is probably excited about the fact that if Danielle can make it out of this town to go chase her dreams in New York, she probably also can. "Sorry, sorry for interrupting. Go on, please."

You would think their interruption would dampen my excitement. Nope. Nothing can rain on my parade this evening.

"Okay, so I was supposed to work the afternoon shift today, so when my alarm went off, I dashed out of there in a hurry, and I think that was when your call came in, Deja."

"Yeah, she wanted to tell you about this whole shindig.

Go on with the gossip, Crystal." I almost giggle at the eager- ness in Rachel's voice. And she is the calm one. Guess this is what happens when I finally have a story to tell. My legs are shaking with excitement, and now I am loving the eagerness on their faces as they look at me in anticipation.

"Now the suspense is killing me. Trust me, if I was the one driving, I would have pulled us over and yanked this gist out of you, Crys." Deja threatens, and she squints her eyes at me through the mirror.

I raise my hands in mocking surrender. "Okay, okay. Enough with the threats already. Jeez!"

"Get on with it then, Crystal. Trust me, I can pull this car over right now."

I chuckle and lean back in my seat as I do a small dance of joy to mock Rachel's frustration even as they both glare at me. Their eyes make threats to keep them waiting.

"So while I was on my way to work, I wanted to check my phone without breaking my stride, and I bumped into a guy. You won't believe who it was!" I say with so much excitement. Not that it is much of a puzzle to figure out who it is, given all my unnecessary preamble.

"Wait, was it Justin?!" Deja asks as she quickly turns to look at me. I can see Rachel eyeing me through the rearview mirror."

I give an enthusiastic nod. "Yes!"

"No way," Deja says with a dimpled grin.

The girls listen as I fill them in on my encounter with Justin this morning and our texting afterward.

"Look at your glowing cheeks. Well, well, Crystal. It's almost like we have been transported back to middle school," Rachel comments with a nod of approval and a wink.

"I know, right, but he looks so different. I swear you guys will not be able to recognize him now. He looks so good, and he plays in a band, and he is super-hot, and I think he has a tattoo on his shoulder or something … I couldn't really see it well. Did I mention that he is so well-spoken, and he is writing a book!"

"Whoa! Back up, babe. He sounds great, and I am super happy to see you this excited about a guy, but remember that you are going to Ypsi soon for college. Do you think starting a new relationship is a good idea?" Rachel raises her brows, worry and doubt evident on her face.

"I–" I let out a breath of frustration, like letting the air out of my parachute, and now I am coming down my high horse of happy emotions. This time it is sinking in that we are adults now. And with all his hints this afternoon, it is clear that Justin will want a real relationship. A physical one. One I can definitely not run from because, for the first time, I want it too. I feel my guts twisting. Just the thought of that scares me. Because I don't think I am ready, or will ever be ready, to give myself to a man in that way. Be naked with a man. Not after what happened with Sean.

"I say go for it," Deja cuts into my thoughts. She must have observed my mood change. "This is the first time I have seen you this excited about anyone or anything. Really. I say go for it. Because like Shemiah would say, 'You are only young once, babyyyyy!'"

The car is filled with laughter as Deja imitates her very dramatic boss. And for the rest of the ride, I am distracted by Shemiah's latest escapades dating a baby daddy.

Soon we pulled up to one of the new upscale restaurants around the riverfront. Deja quickly opens her purse and pulls out her gloss. She applies it in swift back and forth motions. She moves closer to the side mirror to adjust her hair, running her finger through her weave, adjusting the curls and the bounce.

I look out the window as the lights from outside the restaurant fill the street. It is intentionally flashy in a way that draws attention. I am not surprised. It looks very much like a place she would choose to have her many birthday celebrations.

Deja loses her seatbelt and exits the car. "I will be out soon." Waving, she walks over to the restaurant. The moment Deja sees her boss, her fakest smile appears.

Rachel chuckles at Deja as she moves the car to avoid paying for parking. Instead, she heads for an empty parking space outside the park. She swerves the car effortlessly into a space.

I don't have a car. Never really saw a point to it, really. Everywhere I wanted to go, I could take the bus or walk from school to my job. Anywhere else, one of my girlfriends could easily give me a ride. I probably should get a car now that I am moving to Ypsilanti. Not that I can afford one. Except if I want to live in it. It would really make my life considerably better, though. I would be able to come back to Detroit anytime I want.

"Here we are," Rachel mutters under her breath as she finally turns off the engine. "What do you say we walk and go see the river before Deja gets back?"

I love the river; she knows that. "Okay." I know she wants to talk about Justin. Rachel is more the mama bear of the group. She is the one that will list the pros and cons of everything and take hours to decide on a new brand of toothpaste. And I usually appreciate it, but today, I hope she doesn't. I know she is worried because she knows I have been abused in the past and have never been with any guy. But I don't want to think about that. I don't want to worry or talk about how it would work. I just want to live it. Or try my darnedest to something close to that.

We get out of the car and take a short walk to the river. While it is good for the city that the riverfront is attracting more tourists, it can get a bit crowded during the day for the homies like us. But it's nice now.

The evening breeze is accompanied by a few people moving around and speaking in hushed tones. We lean on the railing and stay with our own thoughts. That is one of the good things about being friends with Rachel. We are very comfortable in the silence around each other, and I am not easily comfortable around people. But Rachel is cool like that.

I stare out at the water, and I am surprised to find my mind bringing up a picture of the first time I came here with my grandmother. I was about eight. She had been surprised that my mother never brought me after she said she would. So my grandma decided to make up for the disappointment and promised she would take me the following week but got called into the hospital. At least, that was what I was told. Now I know she was sick then. I didn't know that was the day she had been diagnosed with diabetes. It breaks my heart that I couldn't tell she was going through a lot. But true to her word, she did take me. Albeit, later in the evening. And that made it much more memorable. We just stared at the water like I am doing now. I wish I had summoned the courage to tell her about Sean that day. Every single day, I wish I could go back and tell her about that day. It makes me feel weak and ashamed whenever I remember that I didn't even scream. I feel scared and dirty just thinking about it. About how scared I am that I will never find anyone to share myself with. Even now that I have finally met a guy I am so attracted to, I am sure I will never be able to go all the way with him. And what guy will want to stay with a girl without intimacy? I believe that day will stay with me forever. My grandma may have been able to say something that could've helped me navigate the rest of my life. Instead of the clueless way I am just living day to day as if–

"I love this," Rachel comments with her eyes closed.

"Me too," I reply. Then silence. I decided to ask her. "What do you think of Justin?"

She chuckles and turns to face me. "I don't even know the guy."

"I know, but from what I have told you guys about him?"

She raises her brows in question, and I just shrug, waiting for her comment. "I don't know what to say about him. I can only say something about you. This may turn into something more. Are you ready for that? It's been four years since you last saw this guy. Don't build on the fantasy of what you knew about him when he was fourteen. And for once in your life, Crystal, don't run before it can turn into something real. Take a chance on someone. Who knows? He may turn out to be an asshole. This may not even last since you are going to college. But it's time to take charge of your life, Crys. You know it's time."

I take a deep breath and expel a loud sigh as I nod my head. I know it is true. I know it is time. I cannot continue to let my trauma control my life.

Deja finally joins us with food, and we find a bench to eat.

"It's a lot of food, Deja," Rachel comments with glee.

"I know, right." She opens the bag and starts to put out bowls of sushi, prawns, sauce, and some little sandwich things. She continues to dig into the bag and brings out some chicken, which makes us squeal with excitement. "Shemiah has gone and outdone herself this time. I just hope she doesn't run the store into the ground," Deja responds to Rachel. "At least we have this. You would not believe the ridiculous party favors she has in there. It's almost like she has lost touch with reality." She rolls her eyes.

I take a bite of the Big Fat Greek Burger. "This is really good, though," I comment with my mouth full.

Rachel takes a swing of the root beer Deja had brought as well. "Happy birthday to Shemiah. May she live to see more twenty-fifth year birthdays!"

We laugh at the mocking toast and continue to chat while we enjoy the food, the nice view, and the evening breeze, quietly contemplating the next phase of our lives.

That night, I lay in my bed thinking over what Rachel said, *Take a chance on someone.* I know she means well. But it's not about the person; it's about me taking a chance on myself. Allowing myself the grace to be physically vulnerable with a man after what Sean did to me.

I want it so bad. I want the fun and excitement my friends talk about. I want to enjoy being young and even making mistakes with boys and having my heart broken. I sigh, thinking about how those few minutes when I was eleven may haunt me forever.

I am very tempted to just text Justin that I am sick and will not be able to make it tomorrow.

But Rachel is right. I cannot avoid this part of my life forever. It is time to take charge of my life.

Now it seems like each second is just dragging by.

Chapter Four
The Romance Department

I WAKE UP THE next day to a text from Justin.

"Look forward to seeing you again."

My stomach rumbles and seems to be rearranging itself in weird motions. I go to the toilet even though I know it is more psychological than physiological. My insides do this whenever I get nervous.

Wait. What am I going to wear?!

Deja had suggested the jean jacket and my low waist jeans, which I have rarely worn since I bought them two years ago. Guess it's time for them to pay their dues. I really don't want to look like I am trying too hard. Or that I don't care to put in the effort ….

I grunt aloud in frustration as I look at the meager clothes in my closet. If this even counts as a closet. Is this what every girl goes through when preparing for a date? It sucks being a late bloomer in the romance department.

After finally deciding on a simple brown spaghetti strap

camisole, I fold it up and put it in my bag. I wear my work shirt and one of my usual jeans.

I grab my backpack, which contains everything that will come in handy at our date tonight. Gum, lip gloss, tissue paper, powder, a handkerchief. I think I over-packed, though. Most of the things I packed will not even be used.

I walk into the living room, which is a cramped space, but I am kind of relieved to find that it looks neat and arranged. I say a quick prayer to God. Looks like my mom is still going strong with her new boyfriend. I tend to avoid them altogether, but even I have to say that this one looks like a keeper. Since he came into her life, I have seen my mother do something she has never done before—try.

I check the time again and quickly dash out of the house. I make the short walk to work and head straight for the coffee available for the staff. Downing two cups, I let the caffeine wake my brain cells and give me the energy. I need to get the job done without focusing entirely on my date with Justin.

Rose, a co-worker, comes in with a tin of homemade biscuits and offers them to me. I take two and thank her as I drown them with another cup of coffee and get ready for my shift.

It's usually really easy. The menu is small and simple, and most people already know what they want. In the morning, it's more like a diner. Just simple breakfast meals, pancakes, eggs, bacon, sandwiches, coffee ... Ricky likes to make the most of this space. If he could do more, I am almost sure he would. The hours roll by quickly, as they often do. The morning shift is so busy and fun; to be honest, I am able to get my mind off my date with Justin.

But before I know it, my shift is over. I grab my bag and enter the bathroom to wash my face and apply a little bit of makeup. To be honest, my feet and back ache from standing all day, but the excitement of the date has me all pumped up. In one of the stalls, I change out of my work clothes and do a quick wash of my armpits. After some sniffs, I am not sure I can wash out the scent of onions and other seasonings from my body, but thank God, I was able to nab my mom's old bottle of perfume. I put on my jacket and decide to put on some mascara and gloss since I have the time. Satisfied with the result, I take a few steps back from the bathroom mirror and turn sideways to check myself out.

I am almost done putting all my stuff in my backpack when my phone rings. It's Justin, and since it is five o'clock, he is probably telling me he is outside to pick me up. I let it ring since I am too nervous to respond. Instead, I put every- thing away in my bag and zip it before closing my eyes to take another deep breath. I exhale and open my eyes. Looking at myself in the mirror, I speak with conviction. Something I was taught to do a while ago.

"You can do this, Crystal. You are more than everything you have been through. You can create your own happiness. You can live and enjoy your youth. And no, not your father that abandoned you, or your mother that almost forgets she has a child, and not even Sean is going to be the reason you don't give yourself a chance."

After this affirmation, I feel so much better. It's like my body thinks I'm going to battle, not just a simple first date with my middle school boyfriend. I chuckle as I walk out of the bathroom and stuff my backpack into my small locker. My backpack does not look date-worthy. I will go with a small purse instead. I am about to lock it when my phone rings again. I answer after waiting a few seconds to calm down.

"Hi, Crystal! Are you ready?" His sultry voice greets me from the other side. Just his voice makes me tingle from my back to my knees. I'm almost relieved no one can see the huge watery smile on my face.

I respond when I can finally trust my voice won't sound squeaky like a child. "Hey, Justin. Yes. Yes, I am."

"Okay, I am right outside the entrance I saw you go in yesterday."

I put my small bag, which contains my keys and other stuff I might need, across my shoulder and make my way outside.

"Just stay there. I am coming out."

I get outside to see him in a red car. It looks well-kept but not fancy. I don't really know cars, but I particularly love how it's shaped like a V. He is smiling at me when I step out. His eyes widen, and he takes in my appearance with an appreciative smile. I can even see it mixed with something else. Maybe desire. Just something about how his breath catches as he stares like we are the only ones in the street. I am surprised that I like this. I would normally hate this ogling from any other guy, but I like it from Justin. He is wearing a black and white tee shirt and clean jeans. His kicks again—this time, I am definitely sure it is something from the Air Jordan Retro 1 Collection.

"Well, well, well, dude! Those Kicks are sweet!"

He looks really surprised. "You are a sneakerhead then?"

"Yeah, I am quite fascinated by them. Not much of a collector, though." I want to add that I am too broke for the type of kicks I want anyway.

"I am pleasantly surprised. I never took you for one."

"Come on. There are a lot of things you don't know about me. I mean, we only saw each other in class and hallways back in middle school."

"And yet, we were so convinced we were in love," he says before we break into a light chuckle.

"I am very sure it is not legal to park here. So, are you ready to go?"

"Yes, please. My cousin will kill me anyway if I get a ticket. Trust me, he loves this car more than his mother."

I laugh as I walk over to the other side to open the door and slide into the comfortable seats. Honestly, this car feels loved. The interior looks so clean and polished. Justin opens the roof, and the warm evening breeze sweeps over my face.

"I see why your cousin loves this car. What model is it? I really don't know about cars."

"Oh, I know a little," Justin answers as he starts the engine and changes the gear to slide back into the street. "This is a 1994 Jaguar XJS Convertible. Some might say it is more trouble than it is worth, but only few understand that sometimes, you have to put in the work if you really love something."

I have a feeling he is not just talking about the car. And because I get awkward around emotional talk, I quickly turn the radio to a music station, letting the sound of smooth jazz fill the car during the short ride to the movies.

He finds a parking spot, and we both get out of the car. We walk in sync, not touching, but I am very aware of him. And even throughout the movie, I stay aware ... of the movements from the popcorn bowl to his mouth, how his eyes widen in anticipation of an upcoming scene, his quick knee jerks when there is suspense; it's almost like I am watching him as a movie.

I am quite fascinated and even more curious as to what he would taste like. *What type of lover he would be? What type of boyfriend he would be? What sex with him will be like?* I am not stupid. I know that I know almost nothing about this stranger sitting beside me. Everything from the expensive shoes to the shady cousin points out that the innocent boy I liked in middle school is probably gone. But I want to know some things. And I am very sure he is the perfect person to show me. I can't believe my quiet thoughts. Justin makes me feel mushy inside when usually I feel yucky if it's involving a guy.

Despite the movie being over two hours long and us leaving the theater super restless, neither of us want the night to be over.

"Are you tired?" he asks when we are back in the car.

"No," I answer honestly before I can even think about what it means.

"Hungry then?"

"Well, I am a little hungry."

"How about we go grab a bite to eat?"

"That sounds great. As long as you don't take me to Ricky's." I agree, so we can have more time.

He chuckles as he starts the engine. "Come on, Ricky is not so bad. In fact, I have tried almost everything they have on the menu at this point."

"Wait, how? You have been to my workplace before?"

"Uh, yeah. You know when I got back. I really wanted to find you, so when I asked around, some people mentioned that you work at Ricky's. I went there every day for like a week last month looking for you, but I did not find you, so I kinda gave up."

"Oh, I was kinda not feeling so good. I had to stay away to avoid infecting my co-workers."

"I am so sorry about that. I guess it must be fate that we ran into each other anyways then."

And while this may sound romantic to other people, I find it very creepy and disturbing. The fact that he came looking for me, his middle school sweetheart, at my place of work for days and then ran into me just outside of my friend's home, where she has lived all her life–

No. No. I will not overthink this and make it more than it is. A cute guy liked me and was willing to find me.

Now I am sitting opposite of him in a dimly lit diner where they only serve a breakfast menu. This place is filled with tall round tables with tall gold chairs. The ceiling is a gold wooden texture I've never seen before.

"Okay. So, pancakes in the evening. Never had that, but I am sure it will be nice," I say.

"Ummm ... I don't think you should load up on calories," Justin says.

"Are you calling me fat!?" I ask jokingly.

"What? No. No, no, no, no. God, no," he pleads.

"Oh, really," I respond.

"Yes. I mean, there is somewhere I want to take you after we leave this place, but I–" he says in a sad tone.

"Hey, relax. I was kidding," I say with a giggle and a smirk.

He takes a deep breath of relief, which makes me feel good inside. "Good. I don't ever mean to insult you or make you feel uncomfortable but if I ever do, just let me know, please."

I nod and give him a smile to reassure him. "So, what are we having?" I ask.

"I was actually thinking about us checking out a club that just opened, down the street later, but now, I am like fuck that …. Let's fill our bellies with pancakes until we cannot breathe comfortably."

I burst out laughing. "Okay. Okay. I have never been to a club, and now that you mention it, I am very curious about this new one. I hear it is really fun, so how about …" I hold on to his gaze as he looks at me like he is still trying to figure me out. "… we eat a reasonable number of calories and then hit that club you're talking about."

"Oh," he responds. "Sure. Sure. Let's do that then."

We order our food and manage to relive our middle school days. He tells me about schooling in New Orleans and the Mardi Gras, which I have always been very fascinated about.

"I actually love it. Officially, the annual Mardi Gras celebrations begin on Twelfth Night, which is January sixth. But the main shindig is the festivities build up and peak during the two weeks before Shrove Tuesday. And then there is the French Quarter. Honestly, what made me fall for the city was the music scene. It inspires me beyond music. It inspires me to strive for something that may seem beyond my reach right now. The city has been through so much, and the people still manage to push through and come together and–" he stops when he finds me staring at him. He lowers his chin and folds his hands. Suddenly, he starts acting all shy, like he just realized the extent of what he was saying to me. Maybe he is not used to being that vulnerable with people, or a girl.

"Why did you stop talking?"

"Nothing. I just figured maybe I was boring you with all my talk about New Orleans."

"No. I was really enjoying it. For someone that has not been outside Detroit before, I like living through your eyes."

His face lit up. He sat straight up in his chair and smiled from ear to ear. "Oh. Well, I do love to talk about New Orleans."

"Yeah, I figure," I say with a teasing smile. "It sounds like a city with so much life. I cannot help but wonder why you would ever leave."

He just shrugs. I guess he is intentionally trying not to offer the answer to the question I deftly posed. And to prove my guess right, he just clears his throat and follows it with a sip of the iced tea we had ordered.

"Why don't you tell me about what you have been up to for the past four years?" He swiftly changes the topic. "I have always wondered what high school in Detroit would have been like. My expectations of high school here were quite different from the experience in New Orleans."

"Honestly, it was nowhere as fun or adventurous as your time in New Orleans sounds. Really. It was just studying, doing school stuff, volunteering and all. Well, our football team did have a great season. Nelly's boyfriend was one of the linebackers. Not a lot of action, but she managed to drag me out to some of the games."

"I remember you being on the dance team back then. How did that go? Figured you could have joined the cheerleaders or something."

I laugh out loud at that notion. "God no! Me, as a cheerleader? No way! I did try to join the dance team during freshman year, but they were a lot. Way too much drama. And I had other things to focus on. So high school for me was about getting good grades and making minimum wage, I guess."

"Hmm." He nods his head as he ponders what I just said. As if there is anything to ponder.

"What's wrong? Did I say something?"

"What? No. No. Of course not." He quickly clarifies with a question. "I am just wondering how to ask you the question in my mind."

"I would advise you to just blurt it out. And just leave it hanging in the air," I offer with a playful quirk at the end of my lips.

I like how he is folding and refolding a tiny corner of the napkin by his arm. It's almost a rush to see how nervous he is around me, even though he is trying everything to hide it. From his fit to his sneakers to the car, he positioned himself like an adult trying to woo a woman, but it's good to know some things have not changed. That the young boy who adored me back in middle school has bloomed into a young man that is still enamored with me.

"So, I want to ask you a question." He repeats himself, and I nod again to encourage him to ask away.

Although, I have an idea of what he wants to ask. A question that would more or less promise the best evening or cut it short.

"Okay. I will just come right out and ask. You were talking about school and work being your focus these past years. How come you never had a boyfriend?" he asks, and I try to hide how very uncomfortable I am with the turn the conversation has taken. He then shoots me a sly grin with his head bent and brow raised. "Or don't tell me you were too hung up on me to date any other guy?"

I burst out laughing at his cocky insinuation. "Oh, wait! Did you ... don't tell me you think I still thought about you after all these years?!" I feign a look of horror but cannot keep up the hoax when I see the genuinely confused and helpless look on his face. I burst out laughing again. This time, even harder, I have to wipe the tears that have pulled at the corner of my eyes.

"Okay. Okay. To be fair, I did date some guys. It just never became serious, I guess. It ends before we are able to walk the hallways together as official 'boyfriend and girlfriend,'" I say with air quotes.

"Hmm ... okay. Okay. I get it. So, you are off to college then? Where are you going?"

Justin's voice drops a few decibels. Like it is just sinking that I will be leaving for college soon, and we are reconnecting kinda late. But then a gleam returns into his eyes as he takes my hand from across the table, making light strokes, soothing the aches I didn't even know I had.

I sigh in relaxation at his incredibly warm hands on mine.

"I am still staying in Michigan," I finally answer. "Going to Eastern Michigan University in Ypsilanti."

"Oh. Ypsilanti, huh?" he says with a crestfallen expression on his face.

"But it's a thirty-minute drive. And I will be back here a lot to see my mom anyway." I have no idea why I am going into all this explanation. Maybe it has to do with the look in his eyes as if I am breaking his heart. "You know what?" I fix a smile on my face to lighten the mood. "How about we hit that club you were talking about earlier."

A few minutes later, after some dollars changed hands from Justin and to the bouncer by the door, we were able to get in without an ID. This dimly lit club has several colored and strobe lights flickering around people. The intentionally loud music makes speaking and thinking difficult. As we make our way through the club, it's obvious people don't care that I can see everything happening. Several people are making out on the dance floor, by the bar, standing in a corner, almost everywhere. I can feel the energy and groove of the music through my entire body. It's almost like the music is merely following them as each seems lost in their own. This may not be my favorite place, but I actually don't mind it; it's like the perfect place to let go of your inhibitions, which I plan to do.

I take Justin's hand and head for the dance floor. I can tell he is surprised but still makes an effort to clear the lane for me. I move deeper into the throngs of sweaty, moving bodies. And when we are deep enough, I am comfortable. I pull him close and start wildly dancing, laughing like a banshee and just moving my limbs as much as I can with the little room we have around us.

He takes the cue and has me turn as I grind against him. Our bodies are moving in sync, kinda like we are creating our own music as my body begins to heat up. He puts his hands on my waist and pulls my ass closer to him. I let out a soft moan as his belt buckle grazes my butt cheeks, and his palm moves closer to my left underboob. Even with a camisole and a bra on, I feel the heat on his palm as I sink closer into him. His left hand moves up my boobs so quickly I didn't even have time to react as it glides around my neck. Angling my neck to catch sight of my lips, he-ever-so lightly kisses me, igniting my body on fire. I quickly turn around and wrap my hands around his neck. I stare into his eyes as our faces come together, slowly at first and then quickly as if we have been kept apart for too long. For my first adult kiss, it is every-thing. I've never let myself dream that I could experience something like this, but now that I am experiencing it, I sink deeper into his delicious lips until there is no more air for me to breathe.

Our lips move against each other. Gliding at first, a moan escapes from me when his tongue dives deeper into my mouth. I pull him closer to me, almost as if I want to absorb his body into mine. Oh, I like this. No, I love this. Justin is a really good kisser. He angles my head and takes my bottom lip into his. Sweet sensation spread through my body, turning it to liquid.

My vagina is throbbing, and my insides are warm. This is the best feeling ever.

We finally break the kiss to breathe as our foreheads remain on each other's. I look around to see if anyone witnessed the awesomeness of what just happened. But everyone just seems lost in their own thing, and in some weird way, I am happy that we somehow get to have this moment to ourselves even though we are surrounded by people.

We stay that way to catch our breaths, and soon, Justin brings his head to the side of my face and whispers into my ear, "Do you want to get out of here?"

Another day and another life, I probably would not have heard what he said, but under these circumstances, where my body is still on fire from just one kiss, I definitely heard him. And I am not naive; I know exactly what he is implying. But it's time to stop playing it safe. While most teenagers have already had all these kinds of experiences, I have not. With everything I've gone through, I am just ready to live a normal teenage life. I am going to college soon. Fate is offering me the chance to have an adventure by bringing Justin back into my life. It's time I grab it with both hands swinging.

And so, I spread a wide smile on my face and give him a good nod to signal that I am in.

Just like we came in earlier, we have to struggle through tons of sweating, moving bodies to get out of there. We get into the car, and for the short ride to his motel, I let myself daydream about what is going to happen. For a second there, a picture of me as a young naked child being stared at by Sean flashes through my mind, and most times, it is enough to set me off the mood and make me never want to let anyone see me naked ever again. I clench my eyes, trying to push the thought away. This time, I intentionally replace it with our steamy dance floor make-out, which would have taken dirty dancing to a whole other level.

But I am struggling.

He shuts off the engine, and I can see the excitement in his face die out when he sees the terror and confusion in mine.

"Crystal? What's wrong?" he asks, his eyes darting around my eyes.

I just shake my head and look down, not wanting to see the disappointment on his face.

"Nothing. I–"

"Look, we don't have to do anything tonight. I just thought … but …no, we don't have to. I'm sorry if I pushed you or something. I must have misread the mood, and that is totally my bad. I didn't mean to. I like you and–"

"Stop," I say, soft but firm, as I finally look at him. "Don't apologize. You–" I emphasize, so he knows this is not about him. "… did not do anything wrong."

He looks more confused than ever as he backs away and rests back into the driver's seat.

"I don't understand, Crystal. If I did not do anything wrong, then what is the problem? What changed between here and the club? Because you can't tell me I was wrong about what was happening there. There was something between us. I felt that. And I know you did too."

I nod in affirmation but still take a couple of seconds before speaking. "Yes, there was—no, there is, something between us. And it's more than I have ever felt for anyone. And that's something." I turn to look out the window. "Something happened when I was younger. I don't want to go into the details of it. And sometimes, when I think about it, it's not as bad as some stories I have heard. I don't know why, but I have not been able to bring myself to be close to any guy to a point where we might even have sex."

I have to give him credit. He did not interrupt or even nudge me to continue when I stopped to take several deep breaths.

I look back at him. "I want to go into that motel with you,

Justin. I want to fuck you till we are both spent, and the sheets are off the bed and nothing on our bodies–"

I noticed the bulge in his pants minutes after leaving the club, so he is sexually frustrated. He groans and squeezes his dick as if he is in pain. "You cannot say shit like that to me, Crystal. That's not fair. Especially if I am not sure of where this is going."

"I know. And I am sorry. I just don't think I am ready. I want to. I swear to God, I want to. My brain is just not cooperating. It keeps bringing flashbacks that quell every form of desire in me." I lay my hand on his, hoping for understanding.

He finally turns to face me. "It's okay." He caresses my fingers and smiles into my eyes as he repeats, "It's okay. Let me drive you home."

He starts the engine again and makes the long drive back to my place.

"Goodnight. And thank you for a great date," I say.

He just nods as he waits for me to make my way into our building.

I sigh as I walk into my bedroom. I sink into my bed as I let myself think about what the night could have been if I had not chickened out at the last minute. I possibly could have had the best sex of my life with a guy who looks at me like he adores me.

I curl up on my bed as I kick off my shoes.

Did I just make the biggest mistake of my life?

Oh my God!

What is wrong with me?

Is this how I will go through the rest of my life? Held captive by those few minutes that robbed me of my childhood and innocence. Is this the rest of my life? Not really living. Not really feeling. Not ever taking a chance ...

I don't know when I start to cry or when I stop, but I open my eyes to the rays of sunrise filtering in through my window. After a few seconds of panic, wondering why I slept in my clothes, memories of what happened last night come flooding in, and I sit up. I strip butt-naked and put on my pink, fluffy robe as I make my way into the bathroom on autopilot. Then I make a stop at the bathroom mirror to stare at my makeup-smudged face.

No.

This ends now.

This feeling sorry for myself and not taking charge of my life ends now.

* * *

ABOUT AN HOUR LATER, I am standing in front of the motel. Now, I realize that I don't know where his room is. *Oops! Guess I did not think as far as that simple important detail.*

I squint as I look at the one-story motel, with no doubt more than a hundred rooms and surely more people that will not be happy about me mistakenly knocking on their doors.

Yes! I remember that he did bring out his room key when he was looking for his car keys last night outside the club. Let me remember. It was one-one-four! Yes!

There is a bounce in my steps as I try to locate room 114, hoping to God I am not mistaken.

With deep breaths, I stand in front of the room where I think Justin is, and before I let myself chicken out, I knock on the door.

No response.

Maybe he is still asleep. I knock again even though there

is a pit in my belly because I am not sure how he will react to seeing me after the way we left things yesterday.

Just when I am about to give up hope and go back home, the door finally opens, and he stands with a shadow of a beard on his jaw. His eyes are still sleepy but suddenly come to wake when he sees me.

"Uh ... Crystal. Hi." He scratches his head nervously as he looks around before turning back to me. "What are you doing here?"

I plaster a nervous smile on my face as I answer. "I am sorry. I am really sorry about how yesterday went down. I led you on and didn't even tell you why I could not go through with it, even though I really wanted to."

"Look, Crystal. You don't need to apologize. It is what it is. And I respect your decision, but you don't need to be at my door at dawn to say what you already said before. We don't know each other like that anymore, and that's *okay*. It was a good date that did not end well. Let's just leave it at that. Don't feel like you have to apologize or try to make it up to me or something."

His eyebrows are raised up, and he keeps wiping his eyes. He is hurt. I can see that even though he is trying his best to hide it.

"Yeah. I know that. I am here apologizing because I want to." I take a deep breath and walk closer to him. One step at a time until I am close enough to feel his warm breath on my forehead. "And I am here because I could not sleep last night."

His breathing is labored now, and he keeps looking away as if he can't look me in the eyes. He grabs my hand to caress it, then lets it go quickly. Probably scared that I will run again.

"You don't have to do this, Crystal. I get you have your stuff to work through and–"

"I'm good. I know what I want. And I am not going to let my past dictate my future."

He looks confused as I inch my face closer to his. "What does that mean, Crystal? I'm gonna need you to say it."

Our lips are almost on each other now. "I mean that I want you. I want this. Kiss me, Justin."

I guess that is all he needed because his lips come down on mine, and he pulls me into the sweetest kiss. It starts slow. Then suddenly, his arms are around my waist, lifting me up. I wrap my legs around his hips, interlacing my hands behind his neck. My body explodes in sensuous passion. He pulls me closer, gripping my butt. Still not breaking the kiss, his tongue lunges deeper into my mouth.

He turns around with me wrapped around him, using one hand to close the door, and I don't even have time to register the room before he drops me on the bed.

"Are we really doing this, Crys?" he asks again as he searches my eyes.

"Yes, Justin. I really want to."

I pull him closer for another kiss. I am only wearing a t-shirt and jeans. So, I lean back and drag my shirt over my head to expose my bare chest and boobs. I love his distracted breathing at the sight of my boobs. *Oh, he likes what he sees, alright.* I don't even have time to think of anything else as he bends to put my nipple in his mouth. It's my turn to catch my breath as he uses his fingers to caress the other while also rubbing my nipple between his fingers.

I am moaning softly as a warm feeling spreads through my body. *Oh, this is so amazing.* He switches boobs and showers attention on the other as my hands run through his hair. Then my hand reaches down and grazes his erection.

He grunts in pleasure before guiding my hand back to the bulge in his boxer briefs. I cannot see his penis, but I feel it, and it feels huge.

"Wow!"

"Don't worry about it, baby."

He pulls his boxers down and smiles at me as I stare at his big dick with awe and hunger. He takes my hand again and helps me hold it before adjusting it to stroke his dick up and down its full, thick length.

"Do you want to?"

I know what he is asking, and I'm kind of nervous. I just nod quickly and go on my knees to take his dick into my mouth. Even though this is my first time doing this, I have watched enough porn to know exactly what to do. But not even those fake moans and terrible acting by porn stars prepared me for this feeling. This energizing passion surges through me, knowing how much he is enjoying this and how much I love hearing his grunts of pleasure as he calls my name. Up and down, my lips move across the thick veins of his big dick as his hand rubs my scalp.

Suddenly, he pulls me up into a passionate tongue kiss. He fumbles with my jeans till he finds the zipper and pulls them down. He helps me back onto the bed and opens my legs.

For a second, I am so shy because I didn't shave, and he is going to be seeing me fully naked.

"Trust me, baby," he says as he begins kissing down my neck and shoulder even as his hand finds and splits my vagina lips open. He massages my vagina entrance and just right above it. It feels like a sexual current is flowing through my body as his finger finds its way into my vagina. He swallows my moan in a kiss as another finger joins in.

Then he starts to kiss down my shoulder, taking a detour

to suck on my nipple before kissing down my abdomen till he gets to the vee between my legs.

I have never felt this type of pleasure that is borderline painful as his lips start to move against my vagina. I grab the sheets and lay there squirming as he continues his ministrations.

When I finally think like I am going to explode, he raises his head and walks over to his luggage. He searches the front compartment for a condom. He tears it and puts it on quickly with a cocky grin on his flushed face. He winks at me when he draws my legs to the edge of the bed. I pull his head closer and kiss him deeply.

"This will hurt a bit."

I nod and open my legs wider as his fingers find their way into my vagina again before he replaces it with this erect, sheathed penis.

I feel a sharp pain as he breaks the barrier of my virginity. He slowly adjusts the head until it is deeply buried within me, and in a split second, the pain is replaced with a sweet sensation as he begins to move. Slowly at first, but then he picks up the pace, and my moans start to get louder when his finger finds my clit.

He continues to pound faster as he adjusts my legs and later raises the other to allow a deeper penetration.

A few minutes later, he replaces his penis with his mouth again, and this time, I am not on the edge. I scream … I release and explode into a tiny million pieces.

Justin grins as he strokes his penis, and in a few strokes, he makes a loud grunt as he releases and collapses on the bed beside me.

We both lay there. Spent. Happy. I feel like my limbs are done moving even as aftershocks run through my body.

He turns his head to look at me as we both try to regulate our breathing.

"Hey, Crys?"

"Yeah?"

"You're welcome." He winks at me while nodding like a satisfied cat.

I just burst out laughing. "Shut up. I will punch that grin off your face in a minute."

"I will happily take it. You rocked my world, Crystal."

I reach over and pull him into another kiss.

And we do it all over and over again.

CHAPTER FIVE
"I Am Good Here": August 2009

THE SUMMER BEFORE COLLEGE was about me discovering my sexuality, and Justin was more than happy to oblige.

In fact, his motel room became our spot. We had sex many times in a day. It was such fun discovering new positions. We did manage to go out sometimes. His band secured a residency gig here in Detroit, so they've stayed longer than I imagined. I even went to see them play a few different times.

But the best part has been just being with Justin. I mean, I don't think he is the one or love of my life or any of that sentimental crap, but it finally feels like I am having the relationship we missed out on in high school. Although, the timing is terrible because I have just a few weeks to move to Ypsilanti for college.

Call me a late bloomer, but I like sex. Even though I don't think Justin is the love of my life or anything, I like being around him. He makes me smile. He gets me in a way I cannot really explain. Although sometimes, I feel like he is holding out. Like there are parts of him he doesn't want me to know. I mean, I get that there are some blanks in the story about his life in New Orleans and being back here in Detroit. I feel like we've built a close bond, and I hate that I know he's probably keeping secrets from me, but I'm having the best summer ever, so nope! I will not be poking that bear, thank you.

Over the past few weeks, my mom has stepped up and even offered to drive me down to my college. She is very engaging and so helpful with all her advice that I am starting to feel like some sort of miracle must have happened. My life seems to be coming together in a way even I thought was impossible. It just seems like my life has turned around for the better since the beginning of this summer. Going off to college and speaking with my mom, even occasionally, for no reason at all.

The weeks rolled by. Between hanging out with my friends, working, and having sex with Justin, I kinda had the best summer. And it served well to keep me distracted and not think too much about my future and what I intended to do in college, so much so I lost track of time having fun. Making things more difficult, Justin told me he was going to stay back in town after the band left. He wants to get a place and really focus on writing. I don't know how I feel about that. I honestly did not think I would be going to college with a boyfriend. But it's great, I guess. Justin is awesome. So, I have also tried not to talk too much about college around Justin so he would not feel like I am leaving him or something. I mean, he's never said that, but I just feel that is the girlfriend thing to do, right?

I know I should've stopped working and started putting everything in place for college about a week before, but I just figured that all I have to do is arrive there on orientation day and make sure I am good with all of my classes.

A day before I leave for college, I am lying on the bed with Justin. We have just finished having sex for like the third time today. I'm wondering how my life is about to change. Nelly already left for college last week, but I am delaying. Danielle left for New York a couple of weeks ago, and when I spoke to her yesterday, she had finally gotten a job as a waitress in a deli in the Village. There goes my girl, living the struggling artist dream.

"Babe?" Justin says.

"Yeah?"

"Will you miss me?"

I chuckle. "Of course, I will miss you."

"And we are good, right?"

"Yeah, we are. As long as you don't go running after some girl when I leave."

It's his time to laugh. "What? No. No. I am definitely not going to do that. I love you."

I freeze. This is the first time he is saying it. Although my time with Justin has been very enjoyable, I just don't feel like love is what I am feeling just yet. I turn my head away, hoping this moment will pass and he won't notice me not saying the words back to him. But no such luck.

Justin sits up on the bed. "Crystal?"

"Yeah?"

"Please, look at me."

I reluctantly turn to face him with a watery smile on my face to diffuse the situation. "Yeah, babe."

"Did you hear what I said?"

I try to feign ignorance. "What is that?"

"I said, 'I love you, Crystal.'"

"Oh, that."

"What do you mean by 'oh that'?"

"I don't know, Justin. I just don't think I am there yet. I

don't think it is right to lie or try to fake it. We have only been together for two months."

He nods and scratches his chin. "Oh, oh. Okay. I get that."

"I just need a bit more time, that's all." I sit up closer to him and use my hand to stroke his cheeks. "I told you that you are my first boyfriend. The first guy I ever slept with. I am one of those late bloomers, Justin. I will definitely get there." I kiss his chin. "You know, what we have, babe …" I move higher to his cheeks. "… is pure magic." I kiss the side of his mouth and then push the sheets covering my boobs down. I know this is a distraction from the issue at hand, but it will have to do for now.

"Kiss me, babe," I whisper against his lips when I swing my leg to straddle him. I hear a low moan from him as I begin to move. I know that I have his attention. And everything else will be forgotten. For now.

* * *

I AM RUNNING LATE.

Today of all days, my mom's car decides not to work, and it is too late to call Justin.

I pace around the living room, trying to think of what to do. I should have been on campus for orientation two days ago, but I have been having some make-up sex and some-for-the-road kinda sex with Justin. We managed to move on from the entire 'I Love You' situation of last week, thank God. He hasn't brought it up again, so I think he understands me.

It's just weird to call him now. Justin driving me for thirty minutes to college just doesn't feel right. I don't want to leave him with the thought of me leaving him hanging. And Nelly is now in college, Rachel is out of town too, and Danielle is in New York. I pull out my phone to call Deja.

"Hey, sis," she answers on the first ring. "On your way to Ypsi?"

"Nope."

"Why?"

"Because my mama's stupid car will not start. I think it has finally given up. It's a miracle it even lasted this long. That car has been alive longer than I have been."

"Oh my God. What will you do?"

"Can you come get me?" I ask. I sweetly throw in, "I will pay for the gas."

"Oh. I am so sorry, sis! I am going with my boss to this auction thing out of town, and we leave in the next ten minutes. She really just wants me there so she can be drunk, and I will be stuck driving her back. That is if we are even going to an auction. I think it might be one of those crazy bougie events she goes to."

I chuckle. I love listening to Deja's stories. Even on a day like this. "That sounds totally fun. I will hit you up later to get the full gossip. I have to run now, though."

"Okay. Take care of yourself, Crystal. Enjoy college! I will talk to you laterrrr!"

I hang up the phone and am about to start dialing everyone on my contact list to see if any of them would help when my mom enters the living room. I am instantly disgusted at her lit-up gleeful face. Why is this woman happy right now?

"Come, Crystal. Come see something outside." She does not even wait for me to respond before she turns and makes for the door again.

I'm confused, but I'm more angry and ready to give her a piece of my mind on why she would choose now, the worst moment, to whip out her mother-of-the-year move. I step out to find her boyfriend in his truck. Richard Levitts actually seems to be a great guy, and my mom really likes him, but he is the last person I want to see right now.

"Hello, Richard," I say to him before focusing my gaze on my mother.

"Really, Ma. I should have been on the road more than two hours ago!"

"I'm sorry, baby. The car cannot be fixed in time." She apologizes to me with a genuine, warm smile as she turns to look at her boyfriend. "But Richard has offered to drive us to Ypsilanti."

"Oh." Don't get me wrong, while a part of my brain is very grateful that I finally found someone to drive me, the other side is quite disappointed. I have been looking forward to making the trip with my mom. I even have a playlist of our favorite songs for us to play on the road but–

"Don't you have work to do, Richard? I don't want to take you out of your way, really."

He just shakes his head with a gentle smile. "No. No. It's not a problem. I have my guys handling stuff back at the garage, so we are good. Your mom called and told me that you needed help, and I knew I had to drop everything and come over. First day of college is a big deal, and even though your mom says you are pretty independent and got it all covered, I am just happy to be of help this way."

I know he means well, but I almost want to suggest that he just leaves his truck with my mom, and we can drive.

As if he reads my mind, "You know, I could just leave the keys with your mom?" he offers.

But I can see the hurt in his eyes. I don't know, but he looks really hurt that he wouldn't get to take me. I look at my mom. She has this longing in her eyes like a dog whose bone has been taken away. I think these guys want this trip more than I do. And even though a part of me just wants to spite my mother, I cannot bring myself to break their hearts.

So, I plaster a smile on my face and shake my head. "I am not sure my mom will be able to handle driving your truck back in one piece. It's probably safer for you to take us," I say with a sarcastic shrug.

They both chuckle like teenagers, and I silently applaud myself for not rolling my eyes at them.

"I am already late. We have to go now."

"Yes, yes. Of course, honey," Richard says.

I wrinkle my nose and raise an eyebrow at his endearment. I do not like to be called names like that.

When I am about to make that clear to him, I feel my mother's hands on my shoulder as she whispers to me from behind, "Let it go, baby. He means well." This time, I do roll my eyes.

We get all my stuff into his truck and finally get on the road. I stay in the backseat, happy to be on my own, though my mom and Richard keep trying to drag me into their conversation. Sometimes, I contribute, but most of the time, I just listen absentmindedly.

Seeing my mom relate with Richard is actually refreshing. Even though I have come to distrust everyone she dates, I think Richard might be the exception. He looks like a really solid guy. From the way he looks at her to always caressing her fingers, he clearly adores my mother. We may not have the best relationship, but I am happy for her. That she is with someone who makes her laugh and feel loved.

Right now, though, my mind is on college. I can hardly believe I am really going. I set my courses up during the summer, but I don't have an idea about what to major in when I get there. I have been trying to let everyone think I have it under control, but I don't. I'm terrified of change. And this particular one is really scary. It is on days like this that I wish my grandma was still here. She would know what to do and what to say. It still almost feels like I am waiting for her to show and tell me what to do. Even though my mother sold my grandmother's apartment some months after she died, sometimes I go stand in front of the building and close my eyes. Even climb the stairs in the building. Her cool, calm spirit always reassured me that everything would be alright. It's been almost a decade now, but I am still grieving.

The law says I am an adult now. I don't feel like one. I feel like a clueless child in an adult body. A clueless child that is terrified of being on her own. Being by herself. Without my friends. Maybe that is why I chose to still stay in Michigan and go to school in Ypsilanti.

Should I be a clueless teenager going to college?! I almost burst out laughing when I think that almost all freshmen may be feeling this way.

We are now in Ypsi. I chose EMU because of Ypsilanti. I have read all about Ypsilanti.

The town, from what I have heard, is the hipster district. A bit run down and different from both Detroit and Ann Arbor, but it seems like just the place for me. At least on paper. Seeing firsthand now is another experience.

Ypsilanti is made up of the two main districts, Downtown and Depot Town, both historic areas infused with artsy, bohemian, locally driven, and cozy-looking businesses.

We make our way through Depot Town, the smaller of the two main commercial districts, separated by the Huron River. EMU campus is located in downtown Ypsilanti.

My grandmother told me about this city. She went to Washtenaw Community College nearby. She and my grandfather lived here together for four years before moving back to Detroit. She loved it, and I have a feeling I will too.

Ypsilanti was originally a French-Canadian trading post, where fur traders eventually set up a permanent establishment. Its unique name comes from a man named Demetrios Ypsilantis, who was a hero in the Greek War of Independence. I can almost picture it now. The 1800s. The thrill of starting something new. Creating a new home. Like I am doing ...

Now that we are in the town, I don't know if I am so impressed. I mean, everything seems so ... quiet. When I thought about it in my head, I envisioned the great outdoors, music and art festivals, discovering quirky souvenirs, visiting antique shops, and trendy vintage clothing—the epic blend of campus life and town life in a colorful mosaic. Everything is different from what I am used to in Detroit. The four-year experience is away from my normal.

But I do have to give it to the city. It does look like something out of a picture. The beautifully restored historical buildings, groups of people walking the streets near the railroad tracks, neatly displayed business fronts greeted us with cheery windows and welcoming signs.

I can understand how this was one of the towns affected by deindustrialization. The way it still looks like it managed to retain its charm even while bouncing back is very impressive. Back in the day, General Motors purchased the plant for the production of engine transmissions and employed thousands of people years later. But when the Great Recession hit our country, it drastically impacted industrial areas, including Ypsilanti. General Motors declared bankruptcy because of this.

What started out as once a seminary school, founded in 1849, soon became The Michigan State Normal School, a teacher-preparatory school, the first normal school in the United States outside of the original thirteen colonies. In 1899, the normal school located in Ypsilanti became the first school to offer a four-year curriculum in teacher training. The school was then renamed the Michigan State Normal College, and in 1959, the college was once again renamed, officially becoming Eastern Michigan University. Today, the university is governed by an eight-member board of regents whose members are appointed by the governor of Michigan for eight-year terms.

Yep! I did my homework, alright.

As we get closer to the campus, I begin to feel more anxious about college. And Richard churning out figures about the crime rate in Ypsi is not helping either. I get it; he means well and is trying to get me to be aware of my surroundings. As if Detroit is a piece of cake. I survived there on my own. So even though I nod and smile, I try not to think about it too much.

Since we left Detroit late, when we finally enter the campus gate around 4 p.m., most cars are already leaving. I plan to make this drop-off as quick as possible.

I don't want them to get all sentimental on me. This is not a family thing. I barely know this man, and my relationship with my mother is no better. No use faking something that is nonexistent.

"I am good here," I say out loud for them to hear in the midst of their chatter.

"What? But we are not close to your dorm yet. We were hoping to help you get settled in," my mom responds as she turns to face me from the passenger seat.

I almost roll my eyes at the thought. Exactly what I am trying to avoid.

"You don't have to do that. It's getting pretty late. You

guys should start heading back to Detroit. It's not safe to drive in the dark."

Richard just smiles through the rearview mirror at me.

"You don't have to worry about that. I'll be able to see on the road just fine. Today is your day. I get if you don't want us to go in with you, even though your mother would really love to. But let's at least get you to your residential building and breathe easy when we see you go inside."

He is really good. I see why my mom likes him.

So, I decide to meet them in the middle. And because my mom is looking like she will cry.

"Okay. But you guys are not staying or anything. Just help me get my stuff into my dorm and leave, okay?"

My mama brightens up and gives me a cheeky smile. "Yes, I will do that. And I intentionally picked my outfit today so as not to embarrass you or anything."

"Mom. You are wearing a shirt and jeans," I sneer as my eyes roll to the back of my head.

"Yes. It is a plain shirt and simple jeans. I will not draw attention to myself."

"Well, thanks, Mom, I appreciate that! You'll blend right in with all the other parents."

She smiles extra hard. "Okay, I'm ready then!"

I cannot help my chuckle when I catch Richard's eye in the mirror. Of course, he is getting used to my mom's vanity. She still believes she is as pretty as she was twenty years ago. I mean, she really is. She is vain enough without validation from me, though.

And now that I think of it, even though the past years have been rough because, in an indirect way, I blame her for what happened with Sean, I am just realizing that I will miss my mother.

On her good days, she is actually bubbly and fun to be

around. I mean, those days are far and between, and there has been distance between us, but I honestly wish that one day, maybe when I am older, we can actually be close. I think I would really like that.

We slowly approach my hall of residence, and Richard stops the car. There are several students walking in groups, not very interested in Richard's truck or any of us for that matter.

I get out of the car, and Richard also steps out to help me get my stuff out of the trunk. I don't know why a flash of my father comes to my mind. I don't even have a face to him anymore. It is impossible for me to conjure his face from memory since the last time I saw him was when I was seven years old. Sometimes, I think my mother has forgotten about him too. Not once has he ever come up. I have never asked if she knows anything about him or where he is. Always felt like it was a betrayal to the one parent who raised me to ask about the other parent who hasn't made any effort in a decade now. But I wonder what he is doing right now. Does he even remember me? Does he care? Is he even alive?

I shake all that off and work on getting my box out of the trunk. I reckon my mom will be surprised about all of the things inside that I was able to get without any help from her. I bought the bags and other things with the money I had saved since I changed my mind and decided to embrace the full college experience in the dorm rooms for freshman year. Plus, I will get a job soon. Off-campus, if I can help it.

"Let's go, guys."

Richard's surprise is evident because he did not think I would like to have him help me. Since my own father isn't here helping, I'll accept the help where I can get it and then imagine how it probably would feel if he was here.

We all grab a bag and make our way into the hall. I locate

my room on the second floor of the building. Opening my door, I find my roommate, Chloe, has already set up her belongings, but she is nowhere in sight. Back when I registered for classes, the university sent me an email with her name and phone number. I texted her to introduce myself so we could be familiar with each other before this day came, but she never responded to my text. I found her profile on Facebook to get a gist of who she was, and I was shocked to find out she's a white girl. From reading her public posts where she talks about how superior everything is that she does compared to the rest of the world, she seems like a snob.

We all make one last trip outside to grab the rest of my belongings. Once everything is in the dorm, we stand around awkwardly. I'm waiting for them to get the hint and leave, but my mother just looks around the room like she is trying to memorize it.

Then she holds her hands out and pulls me into a hug. I hear her sniffing behind me. *Wow. Tears. Really, Trisha?*

"You are so grown now. And I am so, so proud of you. You are doing this on your own, and I am so sorry that I left you when you needed me most."

I pull back and look her in the eyes.

"What? You did not leave me, Ma."

"I did. I mean, I used to tell myself you pulled away after your grandmother died because you loved her more, but that's not true. We have never had a special mother-daughter relationship, and it is all my fault. You threw yourself into school and work, and I told myself that was best and was even almost relieved that it was not because you were wild, but it crushed my soul every time I saw that you were doing just fine without me. And now you are in college, which you did all by yourself and–"

"No, Ma. I never loved Grandma more than you. It was just a different relationship because she made an effort to get to know me and really listen to what I had to say. And I am sorry if I let you feel like you were not loved."

I am saying these things, but I am cringing inside because Richard is here. I almost feel like he shouldn't be here now, and this conversation between my mother and I should've been private. My emotions are running through the roof right now, and I am not sure I want him to see this side of me. But you know what, maybe it is time he knows the truth about the woman he is spending time with.

I take a deep breath and let out a bitter chuckle as I refuse career goals.

"You know what? No." I shrug and take a step back. "I am about to begin this important phase of my life, and I will not spend it trying to make you feel better. You chose to stay away from me. I am a child. You are the parent. A terrible one, if I may add. And no, you don't get to swoop in and expect me to tell you it is alright, and you have been vindicated because you have not. And every single day, I wish Grandma was here–"

"Instead of me?" she asks with tears in her eyes.

I can see the shame and shock. What I struggle with is whether I went too far. Especially with Richard. It's almost as if I am not rooting for this relationship. Like I want this one to fail as well. If I am being honest, I don't know how to describe that welling anger deep inside of me for how she neglected her duties as a mother and chose terrible men; one of which ruined my life. I sometimes do not think she deserves happiness.

"What?"

"Do you wish your grandmother was here instead of me?"

"No. No. That's not what I meant. I just feel like she was more of a mother to me than you ever were. It's either you forget you had a child to take care of, or you go around pretending like everything is my fault. I got myself into college all by myself. I did not ask for your money for anything. I cannot even remember you ever taking care of me–"

"I had my struggles to deal with. And you always seem independent. Like you did not need me."

"I was a *CHILD*, Ma!" I nearly screamed. "I am here, without a father, and stuck with a mother who stopped being my mother years ago." I wipe my eyes. "I think it's time for you to go. I don't know what I was thinking when I asked you to drive me here today. Please, go. I need to be on my own."

"Come on, you are not just going to make me feel–"

Richard puts a hand on her shoulder, and I think she manages to get the message because she stops talking and just sniffs and nods.

"If that is what you want, I will go," she says. "I just want you to know your grandmother will be so proud of you. I know she told you great stories about this town. And I hope you have a wonderful college experience. I am sorry I failed you, Crystal. And I am sorry I ruined this day for you. Do take care. And please know that I will always be here whenever you need me. Anytime."

I give her a small nod and stare at my shoe till I hear the door close.

That is when I fall on the bed and just let the tears flow.

When I finish crying, I dig through my boxes to find a good sheet set to make my bed. I pick up my phone and try calling Justin to let him know I am in Ypsi, but he doesn't pick up. I sigh in relief. I really don't want to talk to anyone on the phone. Instead, I shoot a text to my friends to let them know I am at college. It's easier this way.

I didn't arrange anything for the rest of the day. I just lay there, listening to several people pass the hallway, making new friends and chatting away. Eventually, I fall asleep. Hopefully, in the morning, I will have better clarity on what to do with the rest of my life.

Chapter Six

Blindsided

THE NEXT DAY, I had woke up to find my room empty again. But this time, there was a note on the drawer we both shared.

My name is Chloe. I am pre-med, so I will spend a lot of my time in the library. We probably will not be seeing a lot of each other. Just make sure you stay away from my stuff and on your own side of the room. I don't share my things, so just make sure you don't touch anything. BYE!

I scoffed in annoyance at her tone. *What a bitch!* I knew she was going to be trouble.

And true to my prediction, the following week, she reported to the resident advisor that I 'took' her stuff; an expensive pearl necklace she said she left in her drawer.

Not only did the RA, who is also a white girl, racially profile me and assumed I stole it, she insisted that I give the necklace back to her. I told them I did not take it, and when Chloe eventually found it in her purse the next day, they offered to move me to another room, but I refused. Luckily, I had quite a bit of money left over after I bought all the things for the dorm. I gathered all my savings and moved off of campus. I could not put myself in that kind of position to be humiliated again.

Living on my own is actually more expensive than I thought, and the place is much smaller than I hoped. But it is mine. And instead of small, I like to call it cozy. Since Ypsi is a college town, there are no shortages of where to get things like furniture for cheap. I asked around and visited a couple of flea markets and garage sales downtown. And soon, my cubicle of a place starts to feel more like home to me. My own space. And I love it!

Perhaps that is the only thing I have working well for me.

The way my roommate's note blindsided me is kinda like the way the entire college experience blindsided me.

First of all, I cluelessly registered for a bunch of courses that spanned a range of fields so I could be covered for whatever major I chose. Turns out, organic chemistry is way more difficult than high school lab work chemistry. And what was I thinking about registering for calculus and statistics? I barely kept it together through high school. Did I think there was going to be some sort of magic in Ypsi??

After the test, and second round of tests, no one needed to tell me that I was failing and failing terribly. One of my professors even advised me to drop the class before midterms, but I stubbornly refused. I told myself I could do it all, although the evidence suggests otherwise.

Since I am also flat-out broke, I have to get a job. Ypsi is a growing town, and there are actually lots of local businesses tailored to the clientele of the residents of the town. Which means there are a lot of students looking for jobs and not a lot of jobs to go around, at least not those that pay well enough.

Though Ricky has been able to put in a good word for me,

and I am able to pick up shifts at Beezy's. The shop is a beloved coffee shop in downtown Ypsilanti. Every day, they make two different soups, whip up fresh, homemade salad dressings, bake hot, fresh bread and prepare with local products from nearby vendors and farmers.

It is a hotspot for a lot of locals. And a great place to work. But maybe if I was not failing my classes and having issues with my boyfriend, I would have been able to enjoy the experience more. I have not made many friends here in Ypsi. Just a few girls I have classes with, but they have all formed their cliques and friendship groups, and I feel so lost.

One month after I have started college, I head back to Detroit to see my mother and maybe Richard. I really don't like how we left things. She might not be the best mother, but she is not intentionally mean or evil. I took my anxiety about college out on her, and it's not fair. And I feel very ashamed that it happened in front of Richard.

I know he is a very nice man. And even though I will never be emotionally attached to any of my mother's partners after what happened with Deja's dad, where all my hopes were ruined when they broke up, I have a feeling Richard is different.

One of the girls I have classes with invited me to ride back to Detroit with her. Once we finally get to the city, I have her drop me off at Lou's Deli. They sell the best corned beef sandwiches, and it's located in the same neighborhood as Richard's auto shop. I receive my food order and head to the auto shop. I walk around the neighborhood, struggling to find it. I thought I knew exactly where it was, but I don't see it. Now I'm frustrated. I stand on the street, squinting in the midday sun when a familiar truck starts approaching. I quickly wave my hands to get his attention.

Richard stops beside me and steps out of the truck,

looking very surprised. "Crystal. Are you lost? What are you doing around here?"

"Honestly, I was actually looking for you. Was on the way to your garage but cannot seem to find it."

"Oh, that's great. I was just on my way to lunch. Do you want to join me? I know a place where they make a mean apple pie."

I chuckle at his enthusiasm over pie. "Uhh ... no. I'm good. I will take a rain check on that."

"Okay. We can go back to the garage if you want. It's just a couple of blocks down."

I shake my head. "No need. Really. It's good I ran into you here. This will not take long." I take a deep breath. "I came over to apologize. I am really sorry–"

"No."

"What?"

"You do not need to apologize to me, Crystal. There is nothing to forgive. Your mother had filled me in on your rocky relationship already. And from what I saw, that was a long time coming."

"Oh." I don't know what to say. I did not expect this conversation to go this way. It's almost a relief.

"Can I give you some advice, Crystal?"

I shrug a little.

"I never had any children. I married my high school sweetheart. We had trouble conceiving. Then she got sick, and I took care of her for years before she died."

"I am so sorry about that," I say in a whispering voice. I imagine that he must hurt the same way my grandma did when my grandad died.

He waves off my condolence with a smile. "No. We had wonderful years together. But I had my life planned out with her, you know. We even already picked out baby names. Then cancer hit and blew those plans up in flames. My point is, Crystal ... no one has it perfect. No one is without struggles. And we cannot change the difficult past. But we can try to make our future better. Happier. I am not saying you and your mother can become best friends, and that will solve all life's problems for you. But it can be easier to let go of the hurt. It does not do either of you any good. And it will be great to have someone in your corner."

"She loves you, Crystal. She is far from perfect, but she loves you. So, let her love you. You both need each other more than you know."

I try to hold back my tears with a quick nod, my head face down.

"Thanks. I will—I will think about it."

"You do that. But let me drop you home."

I climb into his truck and stare out the window through the short silent trip back home.

When he finally parks in front of our building, I get out. I turn around and say, "Thank you, Richard."

He just nods and gives me a lopsided smile before he drives off.

He would make a wonderful father, I say to myself as I watch him drive out of sight. For the first time in a long while, ever since my grandmother, I feel seen—and incredibly touched when I think of how I have intentionally pushed my mother over the years.

When I'm inside, I head to my bedroom and fall on the bed in a fetal position.

Later that evening, my mother comes into my room. I didn't even hear her come home.

She sits on the bed beside me. "Oh, baby. What is wrong?"

I sit up to give her a hug. "I am so sorry, Mom. I am really sorry."

I sob, and she continues to whisper loving words to me as she strokes my edges.

"It's okay. We will both try and do better. I love you. Nothing will ever change that. And maybe I slacked off when you were younger because you and your grandmother had a special relationship, but there really was no excuse for me not stepping up when she died. I promise to do better for you, Crystal."

Hearing her apologize means a lot. I feel better that she recognizes her faults. I doze off with a smile on my face.

The next day, I wake up to the smell of pancakes. I quickly take my bath and grab my bag. I see my mom sitting in the kitchen, trying to figure out a crossword puzzle from the paper.

"When did you become a morning person, Ma?" I ask as I walk over to the table.

She smiles. "Well, Richard has got me all hooked on this stuff now."

She has breakfast all laid out on the counter. Buttermilk pancakes, blueberry pancakes, and bacon. I fix my plate with the plain buttermilk kind and squish maple syrup all over them before I dig into them as my mom pours me a cup of coffee. It's been a long time since my mom has made breakfast like this for me. Maybe things will change around here, and we will start doing this more like a real family.

"I saw Richard yesterday when I went to apologize. Not that you need it or anything, but I think he is a great guy, and I approve."

"Oh, pumpkin. Of course, your opinion of him matters to me. I have never felt with anyone what I feel with him."

"Good for you, Ma. I should be heading out soon. I have to get back to Ypsi and study for a test."

"I am sure you will do well." I almost want to tell her I am struggling but decide not to.

She must have sensed my hesitation because she soon plasters an extra smile on her face as she grabs her purse from the kitchen counter. She opens her wallet and pulls out a hundred-dollar bill, and hands it over to me.

I drop my fork as I look at her quizzically.

"Look, I meant what I said yesterday. I want to step up and do better for you. I know you have moved off campus, and that must not be easy. Can you just take this and use it to take care of yourself? I am getting paid better now, and I want to support you like a mother should. It's just you and me, baby. Let me do this for you."

My eyes well as I rush over to give her a hug, breaking into a happy laughter. "Thank you."

I take the money, finish my breakfast, and head back to Ypsi. More than anything, I am glad that my relationship with my mom is getting better again. My grandmother must be smiling with pride from Heaven.

Chapter Seven

THE NEXT FEW MONTHS are still rough. It's almost like I don't belong in Ypsi. And I am struggling with money. The tips I get here are nowhere close to what I used to get in Detroit, and I am really tired of serving folks that tip you with just a smile. Like that pays my rent.

I don't exactly hate Ypsi; it just doesn't feel like the place for me. Even EMU feels lost on me. I tried attending some of their festivals, and they had this vibe to it that the Detroit in me just doesn't connect with. Not that I have enough time to even socialize. One time, I got to visit Nelly in Ann Arbor. She seems to have adjusted well to the University of Michigan. On my rare days off, I go back to Detroit, where I hang out with Deja or Justin when we aren't fighting. Lately, he's been nitpicking fights; I don't know what has gotten into him. Rachel has been traveling a bit, and Danielle is living her best life in New York.

I return home for the Christmas break feeling like a loser.

I had been looking forward to Christmas break so I could spend time with my friends and feel semi back to normal, but suddenly, the break comes and goes, and it's time to return back to Ypsi. Except, I don't want to.

"Look, I know it is hard, but it's just been one semester. You have to give it another chance," my mom asserts.

"I don't know, Ma. Last semester was a struggle. I barely understood half of my classes. I just hope next semester is different. I am working my ass off and have been too busy to make friends. I am not a part of any groups or anything. I don't even think I am very likable."

"No way. You are sweet, and you are loyal. I know you are always looking out for your friends. Honey, you cannot force it. And trust me, when it comes to friendships, quality is better than quantity."

After an awkward pause, we burst out laughing. "Where did that come from, Ma? Come on, *quality over quantity?*"

"I don't know, baby. It made sense in my head." She defends herself in a cheeky comment. "But look at me, Crys. Let's make a deal. You go back to Ypsi. Try again. Drop those classes you don't like and take time to choose new classes. Speak longer to someone you just met. And if you are still feeling this way next semester, you can move back home and commute to school from here. I will fully support you in any way that I can. I will even give you my car."

"Your car?"

"It works! And you will have it for free. Richard might even throw in a discount for some repairs he has been trying to convince me to do."

I sigh but not in relief, more like in exhaustion for the work I can see ahead of me.

"That sounds like so much work but sure. You have a deal."

I know why my mother suggested that particular deal. She knows I don't like to give up. And I desperately hate failure. I may not be the smartest person in the class, but I know my way around a good hustle. Plus, dropping out of college will be like letting my grandmother down. And I really don't want that.

* * *

WHEN I RETURN HOME before the end of freshman year, it is like a soldier back from war. More like a defeated soldier. I had put in my best. I have failed almost all my courses except music appreciation, which won't do anything for whatever major I want to do. Oh, and after two semesters in college, I still haven't figured that out. I told my landlord that I needed to break my lease. He was okay with it because he said all the units in the building had been occupied, and he needed an available unit for his niece from Texas, who was starting classes soon at EMU. He let me break it with no penalty, and that worked out because I am nearly broke now.

Ypsi was not all bad, though. I finally started to enjoy some bits of the town when I made a friend. Her name is Brea. I met her one day on my way to work. I was already wearing my uniform when the rain started falling as I waited for the bus. I was already getting angry as I stood there in my evening coat and scarf wrapped around my neck when a car drove past and then reversed again, a move that would impress any F1 driver.

Brea offered to give me a ride. I declined because I didn't want to get her car seats wet or destroy the leather. But she insisted that she didn't mind. Brea is really cool and funny and has a sweet disposition and quirky sense of humor that kind of grows on you. She is from Ann Arbor but decided to surprise everyone by choosing their smaller, less popular neighbor. She is a sophomore studying to be a lawyer.

She volunteered at the park sometimes and soon became my very good friend, more like my only friend in Ypsi. She made it her life's work to try to get me to go out more. But nothing changed the way I felt about the town.

I am still as lost as I was when I went in. But Ypsi did teach me something; I am done doing the most, only to be rewarded with the bare minimum. I figured it would be different when I returned to Detroit, but it was not. The economy was not doing well. And Ricky had to lay off most of his workers and was even thinking of closing the shop as business was not doing well.

The week after I got back home, when I chose to finish the rest of the year from Detroit, making the commute back to Ypsi for my classes, I tried looking for work, but nothing was coming through.

Moving back to Detroit feels like the right thing to do, but it's left to me to figure out what I want to do for money. What seems like a perfect solution comes to me through Liya, a girl I used to work with back at Ricky's. She heard that I was looking for work where I would make above minimum wage. She told me to come through to where she works, that her manager would like to interview me for a job. At first, I did not know what or where she meant because she was acting all discreet and mute about it. But I did not think to question it because a job is a job.

The next day, I meet up with Liya's manager. To my surprise, the "workplace" is a strip club called *Cobras*. There are lots of them now in Detroit. Even though it is day and the poster looks harmless, I know for sure it is a strip club. But perhaps through either a stroke of desperation or curiosity, I still go into the dingy, dark empty bar. There are some ladies chatting in a corner and various empty poles throughout the bar. So, this is what a strip club looks like. I tell someone I am looking for Ali, the manager, and they point me toward a door behind what seems like a stage for the performers, I guess.

Ali takes one look at me and tells me that he has enough girls. That I am too pretty anyway, and he doesn't like when pretty girls dance. "Too much trouble," he says.

I ask if he needs waitresses or any role I can work since I did not come to audition to be a stripper in the first place. Waitressing in a place like this can really pay well. Ali says he is, "Sorry, he doesn't have anything for me."

I almost leave in dejection when I choose to pee first. When I am in the bathroom, some girls come in to freshen their makeup. They ask me if I have some Vaseline, and then right after, if I have some gum in my bag. Luckily, I always carry a small travel-size Vaseline and gum with me. I jokingly tell them to pay me for them, and to my surprise, they do!

"This has been so helpful," says one of three ladies.

"Yeah, would you like to do this for real?" the second one chimes in.

"What is that?" I ask.

"Selling stuff to people that desperately need it right here in the bathroom. I am so sure Ali wouldn't mind. And you would make so much money. You should think about it."

There is not much that needs thinking. It is a fantastic idea, and after getting Ali's approval, I start working at the strip club, selling stuff in the bathroom: cigarettes, blunt wraps, weed, chips, candy, condoms, and more. It is one bathroom with two stalls. When men come in, they buy things, and I assist them with soap and paper towels after using the bathroom. Men tip the most. The dancers barely tip, and they are snobby because I am pretty and make a lot of tips. But business is good, and the hustle is lucrative. Just how I like it.

After everything I earn, I have to tip out ten dollars of my profit to Ali for the club.

* * *

WHILE JUSTIN AND I are still dating, we rarely see each other, even though I am now back in Detroit. It's almost like he is trying to avoid me or something. Especially since he got back from a trip he took to New Orleans to see his dad about one month ago.

When it's been almost three weeks since I've heard from Justin, I head over to the motel where he's been living to see what is going on.

"Hi. Have you seen Justin?" I ask the young guy at the register downstairs. He looks up, probably angry at the interruption since he is busy reading a Spider-Man comic book.

"Who is Justin?" he answers without even looking up.

I roll my eyes up in my head. "He is the guy that lives in 114."

"Oh yeah. The guy in the band. He was arrested like three weeks ago and is in jail now."

"What? What do you mean, arrested? What happened?" My heart starts to beat at an increased rate. I feel a lump in my throat as I fight to prevent letting out tears in front of him.

He finally puts the comic book down. I guess he figures I am not going away until he answers me. "Look. What I know is that he was caught doing some shitty things. I don't know. Some sort of issue with his band; I guess he was stealing from them."

"Oh my God. Where can I find him?"

"I don't know ... in jail. Like I said earlier."

"No need to get all rude. I get it. Thanks."

I made the trip to the county jail. I don't know the protocol for visiting, but lucky for me, it's visiting hours, so I give them Justin's name. They say he is already in the hall with family, but he can have one more visitor. I figure it is probably his pops or something, but I enter the dull, gray hall, filled with round tables and chairs anyway. Several people fill the tables with their incarcerated people in orange uniforms. I can't believe Justin is here. After all of the fighting we've been doing lately, it breaks my heart that he's been in a cage for three weeks.

I look around the room, searching for Justin. I see a couple kissing at the end of the room. I move along and continue scanning the room with my eyes, and when I circle back, I find that the man kissing the girl is actually Justin!

I march over to the table where Justin is sitting with the girl and his cousin.

"I cannot believe this, Justin." My eyes glisten with anger as his brows shoot up in surprise. The girl wrinkles her nose in annoyance.

"I know we haven't been getting along well, but I've been super worried about you. Only to find out that you're in jail and cheating on me."

"Umm ... technically, it is not cheating," the girl chimes with her long, red-colored nails gesticulating. "We were together first in New Orleans. We never officially broke up."

I don't know whether to believe her or not.

Justin stands, looks me in my eyes, and holds a hand out to stop her from talking.

"Look, babe. I am sorry. This is all a mix-up. I should have reached out to you to let you know what was happening."

The exchange of words gets too heated, and a few guards come over to us, instructing me to either sit down immediately or exit the visiting room. I want to walk out of the room at that very moment and leave as if I never saw anything. As if that would make me move on quicker. The other side of me wants understanding and closure. I know this will be the end of us, so I sit down.

"And what IS happening, Justin? I am here now, do explain."

"Ummm ... like about three weeks ago, I was picked up. The police are looking for some people that stole money from the band and think it is me–"

"And is it you?"

"What? No. No, it's not. I mean–" He confesses with a not-so-innocent look on his face.

"And why is she here? Why were you kissing her?"

"Her name is Kierra. She came to town to visit a few weeks ago, and we reconnected over some drinks–"

"Oh my God, you slept with her! Justin! You said you loved me. Was that a lie?!"

"No. It was not. I did love you. It's just that you were going to college, and you made it obvious that you are not willing to commit to me."

"And so, Kierra walks into the picture."

"I–"

"You know what? Save it. I have enough troubles on my plate already, and I am definitely not going to add this to it." I turn to Kierra. "You can have him. And I hope you both have a good life together." I walk toward the door as the realization of what just happened hits me. I turn back around and sneer at them both.

"Oh wait, you are in jail. Well, I hope you both figure out this incarceration love situation." I turn to Justin. "You are a piece of shit. And we are done."

I walk out there without looking back with as much

dignity as I can muster. Definitely not going to give that bitch, Kierra, more reasons to smirk at me.

It hurts my feelings to know that Justin would tell me that he loves me just to turn around and cheat on me. Now it feels like everything between us was a lie. Even him saying that he loved me. I never told him that I loved him back, and maybe that's a good thing. Maybe there was a reason I never felt that feeling.

CHAPTER EIGHT

RIGHT NOW, I AM just focusing on school, my hustle at Cobras, and hanging out with my friends.

I told myself that I was not looking to date until I graduated college. Well, all that changed with a party. The Ultimate Black Party with my girls, Nelly, Deja, and Rachel. With everyone being so busy with life and school, we all decided that we would attend this year. It's one of the most looked-forward-to parties of the year, and they usually require people over twenty-one to be able to get in, but Deja was able to figure out a way for us to get in even without an ID.

And I loved it. The music, the people, the culture. Now, this is exactly what Ypsi lacked. Why Detroit will always be home. I had always looked forward to being at the Ultimate Black Party, and it was absolutely worth it.

Maybe more enjoyable that I had a lot of guys flirting, and I enjoyed flirting back. None of them really stuck, though. In fact, it was all really in good sport because I kept reminding myself that I swore off men until further notice.

Well, that was until I met Andre. Andre is everything. We locked eyes from across the room. But it isn't until an hour later that we make our way toward each other. When we start talking, it's almost like we have known each other forever.

He is older. About his late twenties. I like that. He is impeccably dressed and soft-spoken, but his aura is so inviting. I could listen to him talk forever. His drawl, lopsided grin, that beard, the cute hat on his head that tied his entire outfit together, I couldn't help myself.

"I like how you smile," he says to me as we stand beside each other when one of the up-and-coming rappers from Detroit performs on the podium in front.

"Really?" I try to act all grown up even though I am screaming on the inside. "What is special about it?"

"There is this twinkle in your eyes. Like there is an inside joke only you know about, and you are debating whether to laugh or just smile."

"You are trying to make me more complex and mysterious than I really am. I don't think I do all those things."

"So, you don't think that couple should get a room?" He points at a couple that had been seemingly ignoring each other half the night, and now they are almost trying to swallow each other.

I first attempt to be tight-lipped, but soon my lips start to quiver, and I burst out laughing, "That's not fair. You also must have seen them all night. How is this happening?" I ask as I chuckle lightly.

"Well, there are some people that just go for it, you know. But I take it that's not the kind of person Crystal is, right?"

I just shrug and hide behind my drink. Surprisingly, when I put the cup back down, he just stands there with his brows raised, waiting for me to respond.

"Yes, you are right. I am flighty or a risk-taker. I like to examine my options before making an informed decision."

And now it's his turn to laugh. A rich belly laugh that shakes his entire body.

"One thing I think I have learned is that control is an illusion, and no one really is in charge of their lives. For instance, you attend EMU, right? If the institution announces exams for tomorrow, that will, in turn, change your plans for tomorrow, right?"

"Yes. I agree. And while a lot of things are beyond our control, the few things that I can control, I don't take them lightly."

"I hear you. And I do try to stay in control too. At least over things that are within one's power, like emotions and decisions. Speaking of decisions, you have another one to make, Crystal. How about our second date?"

"Have we had our first?"

"Yup. The Black Party is more or less a first date event. I think the hidden objective is to fix as many black people as they can with each other. We would not want to let them down by not counting this as a date, now do we?"

He looked dead serious, but it's not impossible to see the twinkle of mischief in his eyes. He winks at me.

I like him; I really do. So, what is holding me back from taking this chance? It's been a hot minute since I broke up with Justin, and I have not been with anyone since then. He's giving me butterflies.

I know I promised no men, but for Andre, I am willing to make an exception to that pledge. "Yeah, sure. Let's go on that second date, Andre."

* * *

THE SECOND DATE WITH Andre happened like two weeks after the Ultimate Black Party ... it went well. And so did the third and then the fourth.

"I think I really like him," I say to Deja.

We are in her mother's basement, which Deja has converted into her own workshop. Last year, she decided she did not need any fancy fashion design degree or to move to LA to make her dreams come true. She has been making special outfits for her boss, a few popular party promoters, and some nice lawyers she told me that she met downtown. And they have loved it so far.

"You don't say?" she says sarcastically, with the corners of her mouth tightly turned up, blinking repeatedly.

"Come on. You know what I mean, sis."

"I really don't. Tell me about this guy you met at the party I forced you to go to." Deja wiggles her brows at me.

"Not that I am looking for anything serious, but I think I will appreciate being with older guys instead of younger, cheating assholes like Justin. I am just concerned because he told me he used to be an alcoholic, but he says he doesn't really drink anymore."

"As long as you are not just looking for a rebound. It will not be fair to him, you know. And yeah, make sure he is good. I hear alcoholism can be bad in young people like us if it's not addressed early on. He might end up an old drunk man."

"I know that. I am not a monster. Besides, it's been like two years. I'm over that crap. But he says he's not really drinking these days, so we'll see."

She raises a colorful dress. "Well, Ms. Beauty and Not the Beast, can you step into this? I have to make sure it fits."

I roll my eyes and walk toward her.

"Is this the right attitude for your free model?" I step into the shimmery green gown.

"Just stand still, please?" Deja says as she adjusts the ruffles in front. "Can this professional model do that?"

"Yeah, fine."

"When do you have to get the dress ready by?"

"Tomorrow," she answers with a pin in her mouth as she makes some last-minute adjustments to the hem of the gown. "And before I forget, Ty is having a party at his new place tomorrow. You should drop by. With your new beau."

"He is not my beau ... YET! But I think it will be nice for you to meet him. He should meet my sister and my friends. Best way to get your impression of him."

"Okay."

"As long as you retract your claws. Justin always knew you did not like him."

"Fine. I will be good."

"What time is it anyway?"

"Uhh ... it starts around eight or so. His neighbors are these newlyweds. They be on his case, so it should be wrapped up by midnight, I guess. Why? Do you have to go to Ypsi?"

"Yes. I have to meet with my advisor, but I will be back early enough. I might have to drop by the club first."

She pauses for a second and leans back on her heels. "Call me a worry rat, but I really don't like you working there. I have nothing against strip clubs, but word on the street is that Cobras is bad. It is the hotspot now for gangs in Detroit. It's only a matter of time before a fight breaks out there, and there will be shootings. And you have said it yourself that those girls don't like you. Don't put it past them to do some hater shit."

"It's not that bad. Really. The girls are more jealous than

vindictive. And they make way more money than I do …. Sike, I think I do make more than them, though." I sneer and stick my tongue out. "And most of these so-called gang members just want to enjoy titties and asses without drama. Really. Cobras having such a bad rep is good for them as they get less interruptions. Trust me, it is the least hostile place."

"And what do you sell?"

"Just simple stuff. Things they need but cannot go out to get. And the owner doesn't mind anyway."

"He owns a strip club. He only cares about his strippers. He will so disown you in a heartbeat. He does not care about you."

"I know. And I don't mind it. He lets me do my own thing. And everything I sell is legal."

"Everything, sis?"

"Well, almost everything. Weed is not like hard drugs or anything."

"It's still something they could send you to jail for. Why don't you try getting another type of job? Something not jailable?"

"Deja, I am in college. Full time. Going from Detroit to Ypsi three to four times a week. I don't have the time to work a conventional job, and I need way more than they can afford to pay."

She sighs. "As long as you know you cannot do this forever."

"Yes. I am working on a plan," I say as I turn around for her to see how it fits.

She nods at the outfit, obviously pleased with her work. "Okay, you can take it off now."

"I definitely cannot. You have sown me into this thing," I say as I struggle to get it off.

"Okay. Okay. Wait. Let me help you. Easy with the work of art, sis."

I finally get out of the dress and hand it over to her.

"Oh, guess what?" she asks excitedly and continues without waiting for me to answer, "I saw these really nice pants at the thrift shop the other day, and I think they will look great on you."

"Yay! Let me see," I respond, matching Deja's excitement.

* * *

THE NIGHT OF THE PARTY at Tyler's place is an eye-opener for me. I didn't notice it at first. Maybe because he is really good with me. When I introduce Andre to Deja and Tyler, they like him enough.

But Tyler, who is more like a brother to me, mentions that something is off with Andre. He goes to the bathroom a few times, and when he comes back, his breath smells like mint.

It isn't until later that night, when he drives me home, that I observe the several bottles of vodka under his seat.

"Why do you have all these bottles of alcohol in your car?" I ask.

He is about to strap on his seatbelt when his eyes start to dart all over the car. "How did you see those?"

"I was sleepy and thought about adjusting the seat." I reach down again to find more bottles. I am super irritated now. "But you have not answered my question. Why do you have this many bottles of alcohol in your car?"

"Oh. It's nothing. Just some things I forgot to take out of my car the last time my friends took it for a drive."

"And they drank all these?"

"Yeah, yeah, they did," he answers dismissively.

It's obvious that he is lying because of his dismissive manner. He turns to secure his seatbelt, and I catch a glimpse of something inside his jacket. I immediately reach out to grab a silver flask from his pocket.

My jaw drops. "Why do you have this? I thought you said you were not drinking tonight?"

"What? I wasn't. I had that, just in case."

"In case of what, Dre? Wait. Is that why your breath has been minty all night? You have been drinking?" I ask in a loud tone. I hate to feel like I have to raise my voice.

His mouth drops open, and he tries to speak, but no words are coming out. I look around the car again, wondering how I could have been so stupid to find myself in such a mess again.

"You have a problem, Andre," I say in a small voice that even I don't recognize. "I would not advise you to drive. I have to go now. But please, don't drive."

"Crystal, wait–"

"No." I open the passenger and exit the car.

I look back and find his head on the wheel. I am about to leave when I turn around again to be sure he is not driving. I look over the window and find him snoring.

I take a deep breath and reach into the car to take the keys from his hand.

* * *

HE COMES TO MY HOUSE to retrieve his keys, and we end up talking about his addiction. He says he will get help, and he looks so sincere. Maybe it's something about seeing a grown-ass man being all vulnerable about his pain and struggles.

And so, I give him another chance to prove himself.

Maybe it's my complex of wanting to believe that people can change and be better. Like I keep waiting for my father to show and want to be a better parent, and the way I keep hoping to make excuses for how Sean got to be the sick, messed up man that he was.

Andre says he cannot afford rehab, but he will go to meetings and try to do better.

* * *

IT'S BEEN ABOUT SEVEN months of Andre going to his meetings and bettering himself. I started to feel like things were improving in our relationship. Although it's the middle of summer, I've been spending a few hours a week on campus at the university, taking a few summer tutoring classes. We both are focusing on becoming better versions of ourselves, and it's been about three days since the last time we saw each other.

Yesterday was a national holiday, Independence Day, so the university was closed. They opened back up today, the day after, so I decide to come to campus for a tutoring class. My phone keeps vibrating inside of my purse. I take it out, excuse myself from tutoring, and step into the hallway to answer the phone; it's Dre.

"Hello."

"Baby, I miss you. I'm ready to come home … I mean, I want you to come home, baby," Dre says in a high-pitch tone while slurring his words.

"Are you drunk, Dre?"

"Naw, baby. I just miss you! You are so pretty and-and-and … I wanna kiss you in … in the mouth!" He's still slurring his words.

"Dre, why are you drunk? I thought we agreed that you weren't going to drink.

"I'm sorry, baby. I know, but–"

"But *NOTHING*! I have to go back into tutoring for another thirty minutes, and then I am on my way there. Bye!" I angrily hang up the phone and go back inside.

They let tutoring out about ten minutes early, so I am eager to get on the road back to Detroit. My mind is almost spiraling. *I can't believe Dre has relapsed. I don't know what this means for us yet, but I don't think I'm willing to deal with it. It's too challenging to get him to stop once he starts. Getting him to stop could take weeks or even months. I don't have the mental capacity for a thing like this anymore.*

I get to his apartment door and knock several times. I almost forgot that a couple weeks ago, he gave me a key because he said he trusted me and was comfortable with me having it. So, I go to dig for my key when I observe that the door is not locked.

I push it open and walk into filth. Everything in Andre's place is a light beige color and dark brown, from the furniture to the decor. He is not the neatest on the block, but he tries to keep his apartment clean. I see a dark stain on the ottoman as if someone spilled coffee on it. And that is when I know something is off. *This has probably been going on longer than I thought.* I walk inside and call out his name several times.

I head into his room and find him shirtless, face down in his bed, and legs hanging off the foot. Around him are several bottles of beer and vodka.

My heart sinks. I don't even know if what I feel is more hurt than sadness. I want to reach out and hug and take care of him, but I have seen several people like this on the corners in the city. I don't want that for him, but my life is chaotic enough as it is.

I walk back into the living room and start to clean up. I don't know when I start to cry, but I take a few minutes to have a good cry before I continue to straighten up his place.

When he finally wakes up, I have a hangover concoction ready for him and some pills for his headache.

After he showers and eats, I ask, "Are you starting to feel better? I hope so; I really do. But we are done."

CHAPTER NINE
WOMAN IN CHARGE: AUGUST 2012

I MET UP WITH Brea, my friend from Ypsi, for pie.

She wants us to try the apple pie at a new bistro that just opened up near the university. I have a little time to spare before I start heading to Detroit anyway, so I tell her yes...

"So, how is that business class you are taking? I hear Professor Atterbum is the real deal," she asks as we sip sodas while waiting for our pie to come.

"I don't know. The professor is great. I just don't feel a passion for it, I guess. There is something about the class that I do not connect to yet."

"I get that. Don't worry. You'll find it."

"Yeah, you say that. I am a senior with junior credits and no focus. What do I have to show for three years of college?" I feel pathetic.

"You know college does not have to be four years, right? You should take your time figuring out exactly what you want. You do not want to waste your time and money studying something you will not be proud of."

"I want to just give in and go ahead with Business as my major, but I know that it doesn't feel right."

"But the good thing is that whatever you learn in that class is going to be useful to you, no matter what you do."

"Yeah. That's the good thing about it. And I like the class anyway."

Our pie comes, and we dig in.

"So, what are you doing for the rest of summer? We only have a few weeks left," I ask.

"Looking to do some more traveling. Maybe go to Europe. A friend offered me a job on a cruise ship a while back. I didn't accept it then, but I was thinking of just doing it for these last few weeks—run a check-up, ya know?! It's for older people, and they will pay really well." She gives a playful wink. "Plus, tips."

"That sounds really good, but I will be staying home the rest of the summer. Maybe help my mom plan the wedding. She is totally clueless, and if I leave her to it, she will use hibiscus flowers for centerpieces and serve hotdogs at the buffet."

"That sounds like a fun wedding," Brea teases. "It would definitely rock."

I chuckle at her face, imagining it, "No. Please, don't encourage her. This is her first wedding, and she is terribly surprised that she knows nothing at all, but she is happy with Richard, and that's all that matters. I'm happy for them too!"

We finish our pies and order coffee as we catch up on campus rumors. I love hanging out with Brea; I'm sad that she will be leaving next year.

I check my watch and say goodbye to Brea before getting in my car. I smile to myself as I make my way back to Detroit. Deja is celebrating her twenty-first birthday, and Tyler has graciously allowed her to use his place.

Ever since I broke up with Dre last month, I have not

been in a mood to party. But I cannot dare miss Deja's party. She would kill me.

I don't have the time to go home and change, so I am just going to head toward the Eastside—Van Dyke and Harper area. The neighborhood Deja, Tyler, and Rachel grew up in. Where Aunt Pam, their mother, still lives. I remember going there when we were all younger and enjoying freshly baked cookies. I love Auntie Pam, and she knows it. Never had she made me feel unwelcome, even when her ex-husband was dating my mom. She accepted me calling Deja my sister and is always there whenever I need someone to talk to. I also love how she does not live to get overly involved in her children's lives. When Tyler quit college in junior year to "do his own thing" (aka become a professional artiste), she did initially yell and cajoled, but when she saw his mind was made up, she threw her weight behind him. There's no point denying that when I was younger, I wished she was my mother. But that was a long time ago. My mom and I are in a better place now.

I look at myself again in my rearview mirror and groan. This will not do. I should've made a pitstop to freshen up a bit, but I'm already out of time. Hopefully, the party will be so crowded, and Deja will not notice I came in there late.

When I finally arrive, the party is well underway, and I can see that it is packed. I reach over for my purse and look for my lipstick or lip gloss; anything will do at this point. I find a red lipstick which is a surprise to me because I never use colors. But desperate times call for desperate measures. I swipe the lipstick on my lips with even strokes, smack my lips, and adjust my braids.

I step out of my car, and I raise my head after locking my car to find a guy staring at me with a drink in his hand. I really cannot make his face out from where I am standing, but he is wearing a mustard shirt and jeans with something like a red bandana tied around his neck. Even from here, I can see he is lean with a body of a boxer and a ruggedly handsome face of a rapper. This guy looks very interesting, and I am so intrigued. I have never felt this kind of pull with a man, a stranger that I have not even spoken to.

I break eye contact and remind myself that I am not dating right now as I walk into the house. There are people in every room, wall to wall. Tyler's house isn't huge, but it's big enough for the two hundred people that it seems like is here. It's decorated nicely with silver plates and napkins that match the wallpaper on the wall in every room.

Rachel immediately finds me when I enter the house. "Hey!" She grabs me into a bear hug. "I have missed you so much."

I close my eyes and sink into her warm embrace. She is interning at an NGO in Atlanta for the summer, and I hardly ever see her.

She starts telling me about the several projects they are working on, but my preoccupied mind can barely listen. I coast the room twice before she asks …

"Why do you keep looking around? Are you looking for someone?" She can tell I am clearly distracted.

"What? No. No. You were saying something about … uh …"

"Hmm-mmm." She furrows her brows and cocks her head, obviously not buying it.

"What's up, Crysy?"

I squint and groan in embarrassment. "Okay. There is this guy I saw outside a while ago before I came in. I thought we had a moment when we made eye contact and–"

"Hmm-mmm." Rachel always does this when she's

thinking about something and doesn't know if she should say it out loud.

"Don't do that, Rach. I know. I am not looking to date or anything, but would it be so crazy to actually find someone that really loves me and is ready to be in a committed relationship with me? I am not in a rush to find it or anything, but I am done lying to myself that I don't want to be with a guy," I finally admit with a shrug.

Rachel's eyes twinkle, and her lips start to twitch.

"Now, what is up, Rachy?" I ask, knowing something is definitely up.

"Okay." Cute giggles escape her lips, and her face lights up in excitement. "So, I met a guy. His name is Stephen, and he is so wonderful. We are so in love, and he gets me. He is so sweet and cute. Really, Crystal, I think I have met my soulmate."

It's impossible not to share in her joy. "That's great, Rachel. I am so happy for you."

"I know. And I am even thinking of transferring to Georgia State for senior year."

"Whoa! Wow, how about we calm down and take a step back? You are not seriously considering changing colleges just for a guy, right?"

"Nothing is set yet. It's just an option I am thinking about, that's all. And don't tell Deja about it yet. She will freak out."

"There you guys are! I have been looking all over for you." Deja pulls us both in a bear hug. She clearly has had too much already.

Rachel offers to take her to the bathroom where she can wash her face and pull herself together. I offer to go make her a coffee to clear her head.

There are not a lot of people in the kitchen when I get

there, but he is there, the guy from outside. And he looks just as attractive and handsome as I thought he would.

I stop in my tracks when I walk in and see him nursing a cup of coffee. I tell my brain to unfreeze and make my way to the coffee pot, which luckily was still warm. He must have just made a pot.

"Hey. My name is Moe."

"We kinda met outside, Moe," I respond. "Where you stared at me and disappeared for a second."

He cocks his head. "Did we?" I raise my brows at him before he gives me a lopsided grin. "Well, you are hard to find ..." He is waiting for me to fill in my name.

I take my time pouring the coffee in a mug, enjoying the wait. When I replace the coffee pot, I flash him a small smile.

"It's Crystal. And you did not have to wait for a chance to meet by the coffee pot to find out. See you later, Moe."

I walk out of the kitchen feeling like one of those ladies in a James Bond movie that makes the men chase after them.

Hours later, after Deja has sobered up and the party has thinned out, I say my goodbyes to Tyler, Rachel, and the birthday gal. I really have to get home and crash into my bed. I have an early morning, running wedding errands with my mom. The wedding is just a few weeks away, and we still have a lot to get done.

I walk over to my car and am about to start the engine when I hear a knock on my window.

It's Moe.

He gives me a sly smile. "Again, Crystal. You are a tough girl to find."

"Have you been out here waiting for me, Moe?" I ask, a small part of me is impressed, but I am not going to tell him that. "That's not creepy at all."

"I am sorry if it comes off like that. I just really would like to know you better. You intrigue me, Crystal. Go on a date with me next week."

"Sorry. Can't do it next week."

"How about tomorrow then?"

"Bold, I like that. Let's have dinner the day after tomorrow."

"Great. I will pick you up."

"No. I will meet you there."

We exchanged phone numbers and agreed to meet two days later. I drive home feeling like a woman in charge of her life. At least with some parts of her life.

* * *

TWO DAYS LATER, I drove back to the Eastside to meet him for dinner. We had a nice time. He tells me that he is Tyler's friend and that they grew up in the same neighborhood. He said they were even neighbors at one point. His father died in a car crash when he was just ten years old, and because his mother battled drug addiction, she moved them into his grandmother's house on Van Dyke Avenue, close to Tyler's mother's place. And just like me, he was also very attached to his grandmother and had been broken when she died. He was sixteen, but he had to take care of her the last few years prior to her death. Things were rough for him and his brothers, so he grew up early—and on the streets.

In a way, we have so much in common. Maybe that is why I feel a very strong connection to him.

But I have my reservations. He seems to have a lot of baggage. For one, he was honest about his business. He deals in drugs. Cocaine, to be precise. I don't know how to deal with that, even though I can almost understand the conditions that led him down that path. And maybe I should be more understanding considering what I am doing at Cobras, but I consider my thing small fish compared to what he does. Because even though he is sweet and handsome and seems to be very much into me, I don't think I am ready to be in a relationship with a drug dealer. Not that there are many legit options for a black man with a felony and no high school diploma, but being a drug dealer is a huge thing.

Although, from what I hear when I speak to people about him, no one even knows what he does. Not even Tyler suspects. They all think he makes his money just from being an amateur music producer for up-and-coming rappers in the neighborhood. He must be really good at keeping it a secret, and the fact that he told me on our first date must mean that the connection between us is so real.

There is more baggage, though. Moe has two children. From two different baby mamas. They are both boys, ages five and three.

That makes it just too complicated for me.

I want someone who is single and available, and ready to focus on me, and just me. No one else. Not some baby mama drama or drug dealing issue.

Ever since we went out that first time, we have not spoken. I lie and tell him that it is because of my mom's wedding preparations, and we will meet up soon. But I don't know if I will see him again.

About a week before my mom's wedding, I write a post on my Facebook page indicating I am ready for love. But I cannot stop thinking about Moe. I am so attracted to him, and I'm assuming the sex will be great, but how about his baggage? Maybe I'm feeling a bit guilty for leaving Dre when I decided I could not cope with his drinking problem. Maybe it is impossible to have it all? I mean, look at my mom, finally finding love in her late thirties. I am not sure I want to wait that long for my happily-ever-after. Not after the many mistakes she has made and the douchebags she has dated …

When the wedding finally rolls around, all my friends come through. Except for Danielle, she couldn't afford the ticket back to Detroit. But Nelly, Rachel, and Deja are around. Even Brea makes the trip down. She didn't end up taking the cruise job and instead settled for a volunteering job that will help her get more credits in her minor.

As I watch my mom walk down the aisle to the husband-to-be, I realize that sometimes a person just has to make the best of the choices they can by doing what's best for them. I do really like Moe. Together, I think we can have something good.

During the reception, I observe that Rachel looks sad, and I go over to her with a glass of champagne.

"What's wrong, Rachy? You look way too gloomy for a wedding."

"I am sorry." She tries to muster a smile, but even that seems difficult. She just takes my champagne flute and downs all of it at once. "Thanks. Really needed this."

"Are you going to tell me what is wrong?"

"Yeah. So, it turns out Stephen is a douchebag."

"Stephen, your soulmate that you were ready to switch schools for? What did he do?"

She rolls her eyes. "Well, for one, he has a girlfriend back home. And wait for it—she is pregnant!"

"No way." I can't believe this! It seems as if there are no honest guys out there. Stephen and Justin must have the same blood running through them.

"You know, I am so glad I found out before I made a reckless decision. And there are so many asshole guys out there that will never tell the truth about who they are. Trust me, when you find a guy that lays it all out on the table, you hold on to his ass."

She reaches for another glass of champagne, but I quickly intercept it and make sure she stays on water for the rest of the evening.

That night when I get back home, I text Moe that I am ready. A text he responds with …

So you're mine now, babe?

Yes. As long as you promise not to lie to me?

I Promise. It's me and you forever, baby.

Chapter Ten
Reg Flag

IT'S ONLY BEEN TWO weeks of Moe and I dating, and it feels like forever. Moe is intense, and I somehow love it. Our sex life is awesome. He knows exactly what to do to make me scream. And we go at it for hours. I thought I knew stuff about sex but being with Moe just makes me realize there are more ways to reach an orgasm than one. And most nights, I lay spent in his arms, and he wraps his arms around me, whispering promises to me. Telling me that it has never been like this with anyone but me.

Moe adores and fixates on everything about me. We talk every day. Even when I just leave his place, he wants to know where I am. And I found that charming at first, but it's starting to get to me now. He mentioned how his girlfriends in the past always found a way to cheat on him, and he still carried scars of their betrayal. I have assured him that I would never do that to him and that I know how it feels to be cheated on, so I would not do it to someone else.

He is in Ohio right now, meeting up with some of his dealers, and will not be back for about three days.

The second day he is in Ohio, I am running some errands for my mom when I see his call.

"Hey, where are you?" he asks.

"I am running errands. What's wrong?"

He scoffs. "I just want to be sure of what you are doing around downtown. I don't think you know anyone down there."

"What? How do you know where I am?" I ask, confused, and then it starts to dawn on me. "Are you having me followed, Moe?" I look around the street where I am helping my mom return the wedding gown. Even though everything looks normal, I am definitely sure something is up.

"No. No. It's not like that exactly. A buddy of mine just saw you in that area, that's all. And you did not mention to me that you would be there."

"Look. You are my boyfriend, but that does not mean I have to tell you about my every move. It hasn't even been a month of us dating, and you are already acting like this. You have to stop acting like I'm another girl from your past. If I'm feeling you, I won't hurt you. I don't like all this extra stuff. If this is how you were in your former relationships, you cannot be that way with me, Moe. I don't need this. It's okay to ask and be concerned, but you can't act like you own me or that you don't trust me. Acting insecure will drive me away. Get your shit together."

I slam the phone and give myself a couple of minutes to calm down before heading into the store.

That night, I receive a text from Moe.

Hey, babe. I am so sorry. I have just never been with anyone like you before. I really like you. And I will try and do better. I promise. We have something amazing here. I don't want to ruin what we have. It is special. Forgive me? Please?

And I did. And I never told anyone about what happened that day.

* * *

MAYBE THE INCIDENT THAT day should have been a warning or red flag, but I wasn't ready to give up on Moe.

Plus, being with him has some benefits. He convinced me to give up my gig at Cobras and said he'd support me with some cash for my upkeep.

Also, ever since my mom married Richard, she moved to his place, and although they invited me to live with them, I wanted to give them a chance to be their own family. A newly wedded couple and all that. The sad thing, though, is that the lease on our place is about to end, and I will have to start paying month to month. And that is a lot.

Luckily for me, Moe has offered to help with the rent. I mean, he did first suggest moving in with him, but that would be moving way too fast. It's not even been three months since we started dating. But that is how Moe moves. Super-fast. Like a bulldozer. He gets into this zone where he starts making plans for us, and I usually have to pump his brakes and remind him that we are still just getting to know each other.

My mom has never met Moe, and she wants to. I don't want her to, though. I know she will disapprove of him. She has never liked anyone I dated, except Dre, for some reason. Like she could do better. Honestly, Richard is the only great guy she has ever been with.

So, every time she asks, I make something up about why she cannot meet him. But I guess fate cannot be helped.

One day, after Moe sells a huge part of his cocaine stash, he is feeling generous. Any other day, I would have advised him to save the money toward the child support of both his baby mamas, but today, I really want to be spoiled and taken care of. So, when he asks if I want to go shopping at Fairlane Town Center, I jump on it and respond that I would love to. I love Fairlane!

We get there, and I try out some outfits. Moe goes off to check out some watches, and we agree to meet back at the food court in twenty minutes for some hotdogs.

After paying for my new jackets and jeans, I happily walk over to the food court.

"Crystal?"

Oh no. I hear my name and know that it is my mother. I turn around reluctantly, hoping that Moe doesn't choose this time to show up, already dreading that he is going to show up any minute and make this encounter very awkward. For me, at least.

"Ma!" I smile and give her a hug. I see Richard coming up behind her, and I hug him too.

"Hey, honey."

"What are you guys doing here?" I ask them.

"Just picking up a gift for our neighbor. They just had a baby, and we want to go over there with something thoughtful."

"The benefit of being married, kiddo." Richard winks as he grins at his wife. "I never would have known to go there, and definitely not with a gift. So smart, your mother. I don't know what I would do without her."

He bends to give her a peck on her lips, and I roll my eyes.

"Oh, come on, *newlyweds!* Not at the mall."

They both chuckle as Moe approaches, and I groan on the inside. *Well, this is happening, I guess.*

"Hey, babe," he says as he walks over to put his hands on my waist. "Got everything you need?" I try to force a smile while passing a signal that he behaves in front of my mother and stepfather.

"Yeah, umm … Moe, this is my mother and stepfather. They got married recently."

"Wow. Congratulations."

I see the wheels in my mother's head turning as she assesses Moe. It takes a small nudge from Richard for her to realize she is supposed to say something to Moe for congratulating them.

"Oh, thanks, Moe. It is nice to finally meet you. I take it Moe is a nickname for something?"

"Yeah, I normally would not say, but I will make an exception this time for you, ma'am," he says to her with a slight smirk and a shine in his eyes.

I hear my ma's sigh, and it solidifies for me that this is not going well at all. I was hoping to introduce him eventually to her on a day when alcohol would be present and could help take the edge off my mother. But not today. Today, she is at her full wit and just raises her brows at Moe's comment.

"It is Maurice Jackson. I prefer everyone to call me Moe."

Now I know I have to step in. "Okay, babe. We should be on our way. I have to meet up with some friends soon anyway."

"Are you sure?" Moe asks, probably confused about why I don't want the hotdog I raved about all morning.

"Yes. See you later, Mom. I will drop by later this week."

I don't even wait for her to respond before shuffling Moe

out of there before my mother can chew him up.

That evening, when I see my mom's caller ID on my phone, I know exactly what she wants to talk about.

"I know you don't want to hear this, pumpkin, but I think that guy is bad news."

"Oh, come on, Mom. You only just met him for a few minutes this afternoon, and you have been able to come to such a conclusion about him?" A feeling of judgment bubbles up inside of me.

"I know these things, Crystal. I have seen his type before, dated his type before, and even though I don't know exactly what his deal is, I am very sure it is not good, and I don't want you to get caught up in it. It's enough work to be black in America; you don't want to know how they come hard on women who aid and abet."

"You don't say, Ma," I respond dryly, wishing she could see me roll my eyes. "This is rich coming from you. I grew up watching you go from one dysfunctional relationship to another. Do you even know the level of douchebags you dated and how they abused you? Abused me?"

"Wait. What? Who abused you?" she asks sternly.

I take a deep breath. This is definitely not the time to dig into the trauma of what Sean did to me, but I do want to make my point about Moe.

"The reason why I did not introduce him to you earlier is because I knew you would react like this. Grandma allowed you to make your own mistakes. Even birth a child for a man that took off and left you to raise me alone."

"I do not want you to go through all that. It was horrible, and I am so sorry I put you through that. But honey, this boy surely does not look like he has solid plans for his life. He has no car and two baby mamas. TWO, Crystal! Before he is thirty."

Now I regret ever telling her anything about Moe. I feel a need to defend myself even more than a need to defend him.

"I'm about to be twenty-two, so I'm old enough to make my own choices, and if they're mistakes, I'll learn from them like I have always done. That's exactly why I haven't brought him to meet you. He's nice to me. He can provide good enough for me. He gets my car fixed and makes sure I don't ever walk around flat-out broke. I don't have to ask him to do things to make me happy; he just does it on his own like a man is supposed to do. He does not have a car right now because he just made a down payment for his house. I'm sure he'll have one real soon. You have a problem thinking everybody is selling dope or doing something illegal. He produces music for rappers from the Eastside. Everyone knows him around there. He is really good and will take off soon. I understand I'm your daughter, and you want the best for me. I want *more*, and you know that about me. I'm good! We are good, Ma!"

I hear her exhale from the other end of the line and know that I have won this one. But deep down, I know I embellished Moe's accomplishments. I had to, or else my mom would think I was dating a loser, and given my track record of boyfriends, I don't want her to be right.

I hope to God she is not right about Moe.

* * *

EVERYTHING CONTINUES TO GO so well with Moe. The next day, after talking about the weird meeting in the mall, Moe and I decide to spend a whole day together, like an in-house date. We stay in bed making love, talking, and eating pizza. He makes me feel so special.

In fact, it is so good that I write a Facebook status after

posting a picture of Moe and I having a good time at the park. I post about past relationships and how good it feels to finally have someone who cares. The status said:

It feels good to have a man open car and building doors for you, buy you cards just because it's Sunday, pay your finances, go out of their way with damn near EVERY-THING. Material things are clutch, but later on you start to appreciate the little things.

The post got a lot of comments and likes. And I have to admit that it made me feel good. I can almost imagine a lot of girls seeing the picture, reading my post, and dying with envy. Moe is good-looking and attractive. Just walking down the street with him makes me feel special enough. I know it is vain and maybe stupid, but I don't care. I am going to enjoy this.

A few days later, Moe leaves for Ohio again for a drug deal. He gets a ride with a couple of friends, so I am quite surprised when he calls me to come get him in Ohio. He doesn't say much about the circumstances. Something bad has happened, and he needs to get out of there as soon as possible. He refuses to answer questions about the friends that he went with. Just says that he needs to get out of there, and they are not ready to leave. He asks me to pick him up at an address in Clark-Fulton, Cleveland. I have never been to that area, and I don't want to risk getting lost and not being there to pick him up, so I call Rachel. Her mom now lives in Fairfax, so she has driven down to Ohio a couple of times.

She readily agrees to drive down with me, and I am so grateful. Of course, she doesn't know what Moe went to do. I lied to her, saying he went to meet with a prospective manager. She fully supports me, and if she has reservations about Moe, she keeps it to herself.

The drive itself is long and quiet. I mean, It's nearly a three-hour ride. We have music playing the entire time, but I can't help being in my head. I'm having another premonition, like with my grandmother. Like she would say, I have *the feels*, so I know something bad is about to happen.

We get to Clark-Fulton in record time. We pick up Moe in front of a barbershop. He hides his surprise about seeing Rachel in the car and climbs into the back seat.

Rachel drives off, trying to make it back to Detroit before sunset.

We are just about thirty minutes outside the state line when a police cruiser drove by. We think nothing of it, but Moe looks back and forth. A few minutes later, another cruiser is behind us. They trail us for about three whole minutes before we decide to take the next exit to come off the highway. As we exit, they turn on their lights, and we hear a siren behind us.

"Shit!" Rachel yells in a panic.

"Is there anything we need to know?" I frantically ask Moe.

"Naw, I ain't got shit on me, we good! I wonder why they fuckin' with us, though," he says, looking at me with sweat beads on his forehead.

We are all very nervous, but the car's registration and insurance are legit, so we figure we are fine. I am shocked because I am very sure Rachel, who is always extra careful and responsible, was driving below the limit.

Rachel parks, and two white cops step out of their car. We groan in frustration because we know all they will see is a bunch of black people driving along a highway.

The cops ask all of us to step out. One of them searches

our pockets while the other one takes time to search through Rachel's car. Now, I am really trying to hide my fear. *What if Moe is lying, and they find cocaine in his bags?! Does that mean we all go to jail? Oh my God, have I dragged Rachel into our mess?* The cop that pats us down is younger. His features are paler than skimmed milk, while the other guy who is searching Rachel's back seat is a meatier, clumsy, red-faced policeman whose belt looks like it is hanging on for dear life.

"We've got something!" the red-faced one announced.

"What?!" Moe objects. "That is not possible."

"Well, he said he found something. Then he found something. So, shut the fuck UP!" the younger one threatens.

"We can be sure whatever you thought you found was wrong," Moe says.

The younger one digs around Moe's bag and finally pulls a syringe out.

"That is not—"

"Shut the fuck up!" The older policeman knocks Moe off his balance, and he falls down on the road. The policeman puts one leg on his back as the younger one cuffs Moe. He is still struggling and cursing at the cops, calling them racists that are worse than slave drivers, as he is sure they must have planted something in his bags. The older cop raises my purse up and pulls out a bottle of pills.

"Well, well, pretty angel … are you not sly as a fox?" the officer says with mockery while his eyes beam with a triumphant evil glee. This man cannot wait to put us in jail.

The thought of jail, though, almost gives me a panic attack as I start explaining that the bottle belongs to my mother, and I just helped pick up a refill at the pharmacy.

"Really, huh? You mean you are not a junkie, and this isn't your dealer?"

"What? Fuck you!" Moe curses as he struggles on the ground with his hands cuffed, still trying to get the older cop to move the feet off his back. I want to tell him to stop struggling as I can already see the cop reaching for his gun.

"Look. He is not a dealer, and I am not a drug user or whatever. I just got that for my mom. Check the name on the bottle. It is hers."

He does not believe me—or Moe. They arrest me for having some prescription pills with someone else's name on them, and Moe is arrested for paraphernalia in his bag, which I do believe was planted by the police. Not that anybody would believe us.

Luckily for us, Rachel, who is clearly shaken, is allowed to follow us to the jail in the car. They allow her to bail me out right on the spot, but Moe has to stay in jail. Rachel and I drive back to Detroit, and this time, the silence in the car is tense, but neither of us is willing nor ready to talk about what just happened.

My mind is going 100 mph right now. Wow, they really arrested us! I know Moe deals drugs, but I don't think he's stupid enough to ride dirty. What if that syringe was really his? What if we were set up? Are one of the dealers in Ohio watching Moe? Did they call the police to tell them what kind of car he was in? I hope Moe isn't in life-threatening trouble back in Ohio because I cannot afford to attach myself to that.

She drops me off at home, and I give her a hug and thank her for coming through for me. The next day, I drive back to Ohio to bail Moe out of jail.

The experience of that day still leaves me shaking and scared for black people in America.

Chapter Eleven
Surprise!

THE HARASSMENT BY THOSE cops, in a way, brought Moe and me even closer together. When I picked him up, he told me how he appreciated me trying to defend him. He swore to me that the syringe wasn't his and that they planted it and told me he would never put me in harm's way.

At this point, even though I know we are moving fast, I am almost fully living with Moe now. He had asked me to come stay with him instead of paying rent at my place since we are almost always together. I normally like my space, but Moe doesn't really get in my way. I have never lived with a guy before, but I am enjoying it.

Well, up until I see a random guy in our kitchen one morning, eating cereal, leaving a mess everywhere.

"Who are you? And what are you doing here?" I ask.

He just ignores me and continues to eat. I am about to scream at him to leave when Moe steps out to greet him. I stand here, surprised.

"Moe … who is this?"

Moe just joins him with a bowl of cereal. "This is my boy, Dez." Then nods to me. "This is my new girl, Crystal."

Wait, did I just hear him introduce me as "new girl."

And just like that, they start talking and completely forget that I am standing there. They are talking about a new dealer out of state, and I don't want to be involved, so I angrily stomp back into the bedroom. I almost expect Moe to come after me, but he can be so obtuse at times.

He later comes into the bedroom and starts looking for a clean shirt.

"Going somewhere?" I ask.

"Yeah. Dez has someone he wants me to meet today."

I unconsciously ask in an argumentative tone, "Oh. And how come I have never heard of Dez before?"

Moe just shrugs. "I figured you will meet him eventually when he gets back. He does live here."

"What? He lives here?"

"Yes."

"How didn't I know this? You didn't tell me I'd be living with another person I don't know?"

"Look, it's a two-bedroom. Dez is pretty reserved. He won't talk to you unless he has to. He keeps to himself. You will be fine."

I've visited Moe several times before moving in, and I've never seen or heard of this ... Dez. I have always wondered why the second bedroom was locked. I figure Moe must have lost the key or something, or it was probably his kids' bedroom when they stayed over. But this is just outrageous.

"How could you let me fully move in without telling me you have a roommate?"

He walks around the room, searching for his wristwatch and phone. "It's not a big deal, Crystal. You will be fine." He finds them on the other side of the bed on the side table. He puts on his watch before approaching me with a smile.

"Come on, babe." He places his hands around my waist

and pulls me closer. "Don't stress about that," he says with a loopy smile. "Dez is rarely ever around. You will not see much of him." He bends to kiss me. A long, sweet kiss that manages to make me weak in the knees and dissipate my anger. "I need a favor."

"What is it?"

"So, I did not plan to go out today, but this is very urgent if I want to move the stuff I have. The market has been really slow recently. And I got them ladies coming through with my boys today. I was supposed to spend the day with them, and it's too late to cancel. I am just going to wait for them to get here. Can you help me keep an eye on them till I get back? Should not take long, I promise."

"I really don't want to–" I object with my eyebrows lowered. Why would he want me to babysit his children, who I have never even spent time with before?

"Please, babe."

I reluctantly agree. A few minutes later, there is a knock on the door, and it is Tina with Moe's first son, Mario. She leaves without even acknowledging me, and Alicia comes after with Teron, Moe's second son.

And just like that, for the whole day, I am running after the boys who keep hollering and destroying everything they can see. It's the worst afternoon of my life. They refuse to eat everything I give them. Teron cries and almost brings down the roof while Mario just keeps doing whatever he wants, claiming that his mother said I am a "*biscchh*."

Moe never comes to help with the kids; he dumped them on me. I sigh in relief when their mothers come to pick them up around seven in the evening.

I can't stand the twinkle of gleam in Alicia's eyes when she picks up her son and sees the mess I am in. I am sure she can tell that Moe flaked on me. But Tina has a smudge of sympathy in her eyes when her son mentions Moe had not been home all day.

I collapse from exhaustion on the couch, furious and waiting for Moe to come back. I'm about to doze off when I hear a key in the lock, which means Moe is home.

He comes in alone. I can smell alcohol on him.

"Have you been drinking?" He just ignores me, walks to the bedroom, and slams the door shut.

I quickly follow and push the door back open. "Did you leave me with your kids and go drinking, Moe?!"

"Shut the fuck up, bitch!" The explosion shocks me, and I stand still. I feel powerless and resentful after hearing those words.

"What did you just call me?"

This time he turns and starts to walk closer to me. "I have had a crazy day. I don't want to deal with you."

"You don't want to deal with me?" I ask, feeling even more resentful.

"I said fucking leave me alone." I feel the pain a few seconds after it lands. I fall to the floor, reeling from the burn of the back of his hand on my face. I am even too shocked and scared to speak. I try to leave, but he pulls me back and asks me to look at him. He hits me again, and this time, I cry out and curse at him, which ignites him to land more blows on my face before I run into the bathroom and lock the door.

I lay there in a ball on the floor, trying to process what just happened. My body rocks with a heart-wrenching cry that is deeper than just the physical pain I am feeling. A memory of my mom coming to pick me up at school when I was younger flashes through my mind. I see her with that black eye and how I promised myself that would never be me.

Look at you now, Crystal ...

I should leave. I know I should leave. But the lease at my place has expired, and if I go to my mom, she'll give me the "I told you so" face, and I can't have that. I have to stay with Moe.

I hear Moe sniffing at the other side of the door. His voice breaking. Saying he is sorry over and over. That he had a bad day. It was just his emotions. That he loved me. That they still could not move their coke because someone is out to get him. And now everything is going to shit. That I am the only light in his life. That he loves me more than being alive.

I cry harder as he continues talking, even though every part of my body hurts from where he hit me. Because, in a twisted way, I believe him. I believe he really loves me, and he really feels bad about what happened. But I am also ashamed of accepting his apology. Of feeling like a loser who forgives a man that hits them. Of being like my mom.

The next day, I wake up with an ache all over my body. And the memories of the previous day come rushing back to me.

I struggle to get up and drag myself out of the bathroom after splashing some water on my face. I walk out to see Moe carrying a tray of pancakes and coffee. He sees me and immediately puts the tray down on the table before coming closer. I pull back and gasp in pain at the sudden quick movement. He tries to kiss me, but I turn my face away.

"Babe, I am so sorry about yesterday. That has never happened before. I have never lost my temper before. Please forgive me, babe."

"So, what really happened?" I reply with a trembling voice.

"Well, Dez says he is moving away permanently to Vegas. And I cannot afford this place on my own. And there was that issue with the cops a few weeks ago; most of the suppliers no longer trust me. They think I may be working for the police or something. There has been a raid at the original supplier's warehouse recently. I barely have anything to move and am already broke. Plus, Tina called to say she got a new job offer and may be moving and taking my son with her out of the state."

He sighs. "I know there's no excuse for what I did. I can't ever forgive myself for making you cry, babe." He walks closer to me. This time I don't retreat.

I feel it in my heart that he is sorry. I know how stressful it is to be going through so many things at once. He probably feels like the world is caving in on him, and us being at war with each other doesn't help. I have to forgive him.

He traces my face with his left finger as he pulls me into his arms with the other. "Please, forgive me, my love."

I wrap my arms around him and feel my body melt into his. And at this moment and time, everything feels right in the world.

Chapter Twelve
Forgiven

ONE WEEK AFTER MOE hit me for the first time, we attend a cookout at his mother's place. He tells me that the place used to belong to his grandmother and that she had practically raised him since his mother was an addict who passed out half of the time.

His mother is clean now, and she is trying to do right by her sons.

She put together a small cookout event, and Moe says she is looking forward to meeting me.

I have never met a parent before. I start to feel like a real grown-up. *Meet the parents and all.* We have barely been together for three months; I feel giddy and happy about it. And I know I don't want to go alone, even though I'll be with Moe, so I ask Deja to come with me. She is great at charming people, unlike me, who gets awkward around strangers. With Deja around, I will be able to loosen up and have a nice time.

Moe is driving my car, so we drop by Deja's place to pick her up. Her excitement also ties around the fact that she gets a free ride to the Eastside, and since her mother's place is close, she wants to drop by the workshop at her mother's basement to pick up some materials afterward.

The cookout is actually quite nice, and Paula, Moe's mom, seems to like me enough, but she looks like she is holding out on being impressed or something. Maybe it's because our relationship is new, or maybe it's possible she can see some injury spots my makeup missed. I checked a hundred times in the mirror, though, and everything looked fine.

It is during one of these checks that Paula drops by the guest bathroom to find me adjusting my hair. She leans against the door.

"What are you studying in college?" She gives me a grim look.

I am shocked. "I—uhh—I don't have a major yet, but I am taking some courses to make up for my GPA."

She just nods. "Make sure you figure it out soon. Or you will regret it. Being so lost in someone else."

I am taken aback by that comment. "Do you not like me with Moe?"

She just gives me a short dry laugh and folds her arms. "Oh, child. I just see myself in you, that's all. Lost ... tired. Smiling but tired."

Her words stick with me. Particularly the part about me being lost.

* * *

THE NEXT MONTH, MOE is not able to raise the money for the rent, and we are asked to leave. I suggest we scrape money together and get a small place for ourselves. Moe says he will think about it. I even find a small place we can rent, but Moe delays with random excuses on why the place is not good enough.

Just when I think that we are making headway about the apartment, Moe tells me he has already found somewhere better.

But to my disappointment, he actually meant his elder brother John's place. John is much older than Moe and is actually his stepbrother; they share a father. He is, however, very quiet and standoffish; he doesn't even take the time to bother talking to me.

I refuse to live there, and we fight about it for days until someone gets the place I was looking at. And it is too late to find another place within our budget, leaving us with the only option of staying with John.

Even though I am tempted to go to my mother's place, I don't want to leave Moe. He is going through a lot and needs me. I have been trying to convince him to get his GED since he never graduated high school. He is being so adamant about not getting it even though his coke dealing has not been going great these days. In order to help support us, I pick up shifts at a taco food truck downtown.

Anytime I mention something about leaving and going to my mother's, Moe starts to sulk that his life is over without me being beside him and waking up next to him. He is still trying to get some new coke suppliers in town to do business with him.

We finally move into John's place deep on the Eastside, and I find it very uncomfortable. John is weird. At least to me. He is almost forty and does not date. He does love his brother, but not enough to interfere or care about what he is doing with his life. Maybe I should be grateful he ignores me.

Either way, he is letting us stay in his guest bedroom. Though the arrangement is only temporary, Moe says.

Ever since I met Moe, it seems like my life has become a rollercoaster.

CHAPTER THIRTEEN
DECEMBER 12TH, 2012

MY BIRTHDAY COMES AROUND. *The big twenty-two.* After all the classes I've taken, I should be graduating, but my credits are lacking because I've failed half of the classes, and they don't count, so it would take about two more years to make up the requirement to graduate. But I am not really mad about that. I am kinda okay with it even though I'd rather be finished. The only problem with this is I have to take out more student loans, so that means I'll be deeper into debt. These extra years give me the time to figure things out, though.

My friends really come through for me. Friends from college, some of the girls from Cobras that were nice to me, friends from the other trucks around where I work downtown, and even friends from high school actually send me really sweet messages. Danielle is the first to call me up from New York. She gets all her friends to sing me a medley of the happy birthday song. I love it. Surprisingly, Brea calls second with her jolly happy birthday song. It is extra cute. And Nelly follows it with the sweet video of us over the years, including when we did the Janet Jackson choreography. I don't even know where she found it, but it is the sweetest thing. Nelly, Rachel, and Deja then throw me a birthday party at Deja's place.

I can tell Moe's mood is sour. Since the morning when the text messages and calls started coming in. He says he got me the best gift, though, and that I will have my mind blown. In my heart, I do plan to be enthusiastic about the gift and declare it the best I have ever gotten. I think he needs validation.

During the party, I see Moe snorting coke outside.

"What are you doing?" My jaw drops in surprise. I never knew Moe was using. That explains some of his behavior lately. *What have I gotten myself into?*

"What does it look like?" he responds with so much anger in his tone.

"I really wish you would not do that here. You know Deja does not like having that kind of shit in her space."

"Well, fuck Deja. I am a grown man. I can do whatever I want." I know he means me nagging him to get a job. A customer of mine had mentioned some job vacancies, so I have been trying to get him to apply.

"You cannot say that about her," I shush him. "That–"

"You know what? Fuck you too! Do you think I have not seen those messages sent by them dudes in your phone? Huh? Is that what you are doing now? Giving it to everybody?"

I bring out my phone. "What is wrong with you? Going through my phone? What the fuck, Moe? And they are just friends. You know you are the only one I want."

He grabs the phone from me, and before I can blink, he slams it on the ground before walking back into Deja's place.

I fall to the ground and pick up the broken phone. I wipe the tears off my face so nobody would notice when Nelly calls my name, and I go back inside to find the gift Moe had got me. It was a bird. A Cockatiel; one of my favorite kinds of pet birds. I love the gift, so I do show enthusiasm and gratitude.

As the party goes on, Moe still walks around with his face bent out of shape, still upset about what he thinks he saw on my phone.

He doesn't wait till the end of the party to leave; he just does. Normally that would've upset me, but I'm okay with it because I need some time away from him. So, I let him go without making a big deal about it and continue to enjoy my party. I manage to hide the broken phone from all of my friends.

This time, Moe doesn't apologize for what he did or even offer to pay for me to get my phone fixed when I do a week later. I feel defeated in this relationship. I know he can do better than this. Everyone knows Moe and I have been going steady. *How would I look if I don't even try to work it out? To be honest, I don't even know where to start. I want to ask Deja, Nelly, or Rachel what I should do, but I don't want to answer all the questions I know that will come with letting them in our business now. It may be better if I show him how to love me!*

I work through the holidays and make a lot more tips. I only manage to drop by Ma's on Christmas Eve for dinner. I can tell she is not happy about my living arrangement, but she is trying her best not to push. It's probably thanks to Richard that she has backed off bringing it up. I am sure if they knew Moe hit me, Richard would be the first to flatten him with a bullet while my mother pushed me out of that place.

I intentionally throw myself into work, which is my coping mechanism. I only come home to check on Doogie, my Cockatiel. He is the sweetest bird. Affectionate and never shy about showing me love by snuggling and showering me with kisses.

The new year rolls by, and Moe keeps saying he has a plan to get us out of his brother's place. Every time he mentions it, it sounds like a broken record to me. I just don't see him making any progress to ensure that we are able to secure a place on our own.

CHAPTER FOURTEEN
JANUARY 16TH, 2013

AFTER A STRESSFUL DAY at work, I come home and am surprised Moe is in the room watching TV and not out running the streets. Doogie immediately comes to perch on my shoulder and starts humming the tune I taught him, which is actually just a silly ad song I like.

After taking a shower, I walk into the bedroom and see Moe with my phone in his hand.

"No. You don't get to touch my phone after you destroyed it without apologizing," I say as I try to reach for the phone.

But he only rolls off the bed, and I can see he is scrolling through my messages.

"Who is Dre?"

I exhale, already sensing trouble ahead.

"He is a friend," I respond, trying not to let my voice shake so he can't sense my fear.

"A friend you dated, huh?"

"Yes," I answer honestly. "I was with him before I met you last year. But he had a drinking problem and was not ready to get help, so we broke up."

The irony is not lost on me that I left Dre to be with someone like Moe. My poor choice of men will definitely be my undoing.

I must have blanked out because when Moe calls my name again, he is holding Doogie, and my heart starts beating faster.

"Let Doogie go, Moe."

"Got your attention, didn't it?"

"What do you want? I met with Dre recently when he came by the food truck, and we talked about his recovery and how well he is doing. Read the chat. You will see there is nothing there."

"Now. Now. You know that is not the point," Moe says in a low tone with that crazy evil gleam he had in his eyes before he slammed my phone on my birthday. I am beginning to recognize it as a precursor to his madness.

"The point is, Crystal, you have been texting your ex. And lied to me about it."

"I did not lie. You asked, and I answered."

"How about I let you think about how hurt I am now finding out that the girl I love is trying to cheat on me. Let me just help you understand what will happen if you do dare to cheat on me, Crystal."

Moe grabs Doogie's cage and heads for the front door in a rage. His evil gleam does not subside. I know he'll do it. He knows how attached I have grown to Doogie. I never had pets growing up, even though I really wanted one. And I proposed a bird to my mother back then because it was low mainte-nance and still capable of having some sort of interaction.

But Moe knew exactly what he was doing when he gave me Doogie for my birthday. It was for a day like this.

"Don't do anything to Doogie, Moe," I plead and try to

get closer to rescue my bird. But I am too late. Doogie falls to the ground. I rush to his tiny limp body as his fragile neck has been broken. I just sit back on my heels and stare at Moe with so much hatred in my eyes.

"Don't test me, Crystal," he warns and walks out of the room with my car keys.

I lay with my dead bird on my lap—all cried out. And for a split second, I hate that my grandmother ever told the story of how she met my grandfather. I wish I never knew something so beautiful and pure existed. Maybe it would have been better to cope with this crazy situation. But I know it. I know in my heart that it can be better for me. But I can't leave now. Not with Moe on this psychotic bend. He could do something drastic to me. I am stuck in this. I can only sulk about my situation as I sit and think to myself, *"What am I going to do about any of this?"* Little do I know, this is just the beginning.

* * *

"BRRRING-BRRRING-BRRRING." THE sound of my alarm startles me. A ray of light almost blinds me as I try to open my eyes to grab my phone to hit the snooze button and check the time. I was supposed to wake up an hour ago for classes. I must've slept through the alarm when it first went off. When I walk to the bathroom, Moe is asleep on the couch, so I quietly and quickly shower, get dressed, grab my keys, and head out.

As I am in my car heading to Ypsi, it cuts off in the middle of the road. It refuses to start back up, and I can't figure out the cause. I think of calling Moe, but how would he get to me? So, I call Dre, and he tells me to just sit tight, and he'll be pulling up in fifteen minutes. When he arrives, he checks under the hood and under the car to see what the problem could be. When he finishes diagnosing the car, he tells me that my spark plugs have been snatched out, and there are some holes in a couple of the hoses under the car. He says they look purposefully inflicted and that it might cost a few hundred to get the hoses replaced.

The last thing I want to spend my money on is a mechanic, and I really don't want to go to Richard and risk him figuring out that Moe may have a hand in this.

So, I do something that is totally stupid but manages to pay off. I have insurance on my car, so I get a tow truck to take it to a junkyard where my cousin Novi works. I remember her mentioning during my birthday party that her boss knows how to make a car disappear so people can claim their insurance on it.

I give her a call, and she says she can help. I tell her to hold off on the crushing until I am sure I will be able to get my claim. Then I call the insurance company and report my car stolen. They immediately get me a rental car to use while they investigate.

I am stressed, and my day has been long. Despite everything Moe is putting me through, I know he loves me, and I love him too. I want to talk to him about getting some help. Maybe that way, we can be happy without arguing and fighting all the time, but we won't talk tonight because I am too upset to even look at him. I am not even going to say anything to him about the car. I am just going to pull up in the rental and try to ignore the fact that he is being a monster right now. When I get back home later that evening, I walk into another disaster. Moe had soaked my laptop in water. Intentionally to destroy it, knowing how important the laptop is for college. I scream in frustration when I observe that he is not home to explain the reason for this. I will have to dig out of the money for college to get another one.

My phone beeps and I see a message from Nelly. It's just:

??

And then it hits me, with everything happening with Moe, I actually forgot all about my best friend's birthday. Oh my God, Nelly's probably so upset with me. This has never happened before. We always celebrate it together.

I quickly call her to apologize for being a bad friend. We have a long conversation, and I do end up mentioning some things about what has been going on between me and Moe, but not everything. I have never told anyone about this except her. I can hear it in her voice that she's heartbroken from the things I'm telling her. For her to know that her best friend has been dealing with such foolishness. We start crying together, and she begs me to leave Moe before he does something to hurt me or take me away from them. She suggests I call the cops on him, but I tell her that I won't do that to him. She calls me "stupid," but I tell her I don't think it is a good idea right now. Besides, I know how much he hates cops, and it could make him angrier.

For the next few days, Moe and I avoid each other as much as we can. But Moe sometimes still ends up taking the rental car, forcing me to figure out transportation to Ypsi.

Sometimes to get to school, Richard gives me a ride and then picks me up from school. He has restoration work he is doing for a client in Ypsi, so he helps me out. And I am so very grateful.

That is until Moe starts accusing me of more cheating. He is suspicious about my relationship with Richard, even going far enough to allege that I am sleeping with my stepfather. I can't take his allegations anymore, so when he offers to drive me to school the week after, I accept.

I stay silent even as I can see him stealing glances and trying to start a conversation. I give him a one-word response to show my displeasure at his motive for offering to drive me. We had a conversation about him driving me to school in the past so he could keep my car to *handle his business.* I told him that it was a stupid idea because it would put too many miles on the car for no reason. Not only that, but by the time he dropped me off, it'd be time to come back and get me in just a few hours. I don't mention that conversation this time. I just shut up and ride.

Moe reaches into his pockets and pulls out a pack of Twizzlers. Smiling sheepishly before offering it to me like a prize.

I shake my head in refusal.

"Just take it, Crys. I know you love this stuff. I got it for you."

"Actually, you're wrong. I am over Twizzlers. Richard has got me addicted to Skittles now."

I know the second after I finish the sentence that I should not have said that. Just the mention of Richard's name is a trigger for him.

Nothing prepares me for the repercussions, though.

Moe squeezes the candy and throws it out the window. Fuming as he grips the wheel with both hands. He starts driving up the I-94 highway erratically. Pumping up the gas, saying he will kill us both. As he increases the speed, my heart starts racing. I begin to think as he is still focused on pushing the speed limit. I reach for my phone and text Tyler, asking him to call Moe and help me.

When I get no response, I realize it's just me for myself. I silently pray for a police car to flag him down for exceeding the speed limit. No such luck.

I am the only one that can save me now.

Before I can even think of what to say, we are coming up off the highway. Moe pulls over sharply to the side of a deserted road. He switches off the engine and reaches into his waistband to pull out his gun, and threatens to take my life.

I manage to simmer down my anger and fear and try to sweet talk my way out of it by telling him how much I love him and only him; that things will work out between us. And we can be happy again and be a team again like we used to be. I promise him that we will start over fresh, where we can be friends and lovers.

Knowing my life is hanging by a thread, I almost cry in relief when he manages to put down the gun while promising to be a better boyfriend.

I smile to let him think I am happy about his decision and quickly lean over to hug and give him a kiss. All the while screaming in my head. *This is enough ... I can't take it anymore! I have to get out of here! He's sick in the head. Though, I know he will make it an ugly nightmare when I try to leave.*

He drives us back home in silence, even as I can see him smiling cheekily like a little kid who got his first taste of ice cream. Looks like I am going to miss my classes today.

While he goes to find a place to park the car, I rush into the house and make for the bedroom, where I take my wallet and important documents to the bathroom and hide them under the sink so that Moe can't find them. With what he pulled today, I know I just narrowly escaped death this time. And I may not be so lucky next time. Hitting me, manipulating me, and destroying my things to sabotage me may be bad, but none of that matters if he manages to kill me. I cannot do that to myself. I cannot do that to my mother, my grandmother, or my friends. They deserve better than me being killed in an abusive relationship. I can almost imagine my grandmother being so disappointed in where I am right now.

I finally come to terms with what almost happened today, and I start shaking. I turn on the shower and let it run before I break down and cry. I step into the hot shower with full clothes. I crouch and wrap my arms around my shoulders as hot water splashes on my body. I let myself have a good cry before standing up, wiping my tears, and finally taking off my clothes as I strategize an escape plan. All I can think about now is me and Nelly crying on the phone together and listening to the sorrow in her voice while she begged me to leave Moe. I am going to get away from him somehow.

When I come out of the shower, I find him in the room asleep. It's a little early, so I just lay down and watch Criminal Minds reruns on TV until my eyes get heavy. I say a quick prayer to God because I might as well take the gun and shoot myself if he tries to touch me tonight. I check his usual hiding spot for the gun to hide it elsewhere, but he must have already hidden it somewhere new.

I crawl onto the edge of the bed and watch TV until I manage to shut my eyes. Luckily for me, I am blessed with a dreamless sleep as I slip into the abyss.

The next morning, I am up before dawn. I take a shower and put my important stuff in my backpack. I am almost ready to leave when Moe wakes up drowsily, and I fake a wide smile. I walk across the room to give him a kiss after he sits up, hoping my smile does not crack, or he will sense that I am up to something.

"Hey, babe. Good morning," he greets as if he has completely forgotten almost ending both our lives yesterday.

"I was thinking we should go out and get some waffles. I have some plans for the future I want to share with you."

"Oh really. That's awesome. But since I missed class yesterday, I can't miss today because I have a test, but I was also thinking about making some of my Cracker Barrel chicken and dumplings tonight."

"Oh, that's great."

"Hmm-mmm. I will pick up some groceries on my way back from school."

"Sure, babe." He kisses me again, and I manage to keep my smile and say, "Love you!" with all the enthusiasm I can muster.

"Love you too, babe."

I grab my keys and count my steps to the door with my heart beating so loud in my ears. I do not stop counting till I get inside my car and drive into freedom.

* * *

I HEAD STRAIGHT TO my mother's house and breakdown in her arms. I finally tell her and Richard everything that has been going on with me and Moe over the past months. Richard is so mad he almost gets into his truck to go put a bullet into Moe, but my mom calms him down and reminds him that we have too much to lose to act reckless and to think it through first.

Instead of judging my decisions, my mom just hugs me and tells me that it is important to make a police report so I can get a restraining order against him because she is so sure he will try to come back for me.

We go to the police station, and I give my statement. Then, I head downtown to the Clerk's Office and file for a restraining order. True to my mother's words, that evening, after he must have figured that I am not coming back to him, Moe comes to my mother's place and starts screaming threats. Saying he will kill my mother and Richard and my friends and everyone I care about. I am so scared; I almost go outside to speak with him and beg or even follow him home just to ensure the safety of the people I love, but my mother helps me realize that is exactly what he wants. For me to be afraid. Richard is about to go out and face him when he throws a brick through one of the bedroom windows. This time, I am the one who reminds him that Moe has a fully loaded gun and is very capable of using it.

Instead, we lock all doors and call the police. Moe is arrested for public disturbance and destruction of private property. I know how scared he is of prison because he already has two strikes. I hate that I have to watch over my shoulder every time I leave the house now. A part of me is mad that I feel like I need a man to protect me, but then I just bask in the grace that I am not alone in this. Even though it started out like that, I am more than happy to realize that I have people around me that will come through for me.

* * *

MOE EVENTUALLY MADE BAIL, and I found out soon after that the restraining order was not enough to keep him away. Every time I changed my number, he always managed to get it and would send threats. Saying he would send someone to shoot me in the head and would throw acid in my face so nobody else would want me.

I started to have sleepless nights and decided to take a whole semester off school because I could not focus. I was mentally drained and felt like I was going crazy. I even considered hiring a hitman to kill him before he killed me.

But I was talked out of it by my mother. Advising me not to stoop to the level of the criminal that he is.

A few weeks after I left him, Moe decided to try and ruin my reputation by leaking nude pictures of me on Instagram. When he called from a phone number I didn't recognize, I begged him to remove them, but he told me that he would do whatever he needed to do to ruin my life because I ruined his. For weeks, I couldn't face anyone. But then my girls came through for me and advised me to hold my head high. They said he had played all his cards and lost. Plus, the pictures looked really good, so any future beau would know just how lucky he was going to be.

I laughed at that comment made by Nelly. She is the best. Even though the night Moe had killed Doogie was her birthday, and I was too engrossed in my drama to remember or celebrate her, she understood and still stood by me through the whole nude-pictures-embarrassing phase. To make it up to her, when I finally got the courage to leave the house, the first place I went was to spend time with her.

After a few more months went by, he started to back off with the threats. And soon, it was all pathetic pleas for me to take him back. That he is now better, and he is sorry.

I continued to ignore his calls and text messages and continued blocking all of his numbers. For me, he is a part of my past. The most turbulent phase of my life that I wish I could blot out, but I cannot. Instead, I get to relive every assault and trauma I went through with him. But I managed to gain something out of the experience with Moe. When the threats faded and I was mentally able to go back to college, it was with a clear vision of what I wanted to major in.

I started back to school more focused than ever. It was a breeze. And two years later, I graduated from college with a *bachelor's degree* in Criminal Justice and Criminology.

About a year after the relationship ended, I received a phone call from a female saying that Moe had been abusing her and threatening her family. She was crying and asking me for advice on how to make him leave her alone. I didn't know who she was, but I recognized the fear in her voice. I also had that. So even though I didn't know how she got my number, my advice for her was only one word—run!

January 2022

I SIP MY COFFEE while loving how warm it feels in my hands. No matter how much I love, and I am grateful for a winter Christmas, I will probably never love the cold weather. I walk briskly as I near my office building where I work as a prosecutor with the Department of Justice.

I love my job. I love my family. I recently gave my mother and Richard an anniversary trip to Rome. My mother is obsessed with Rome. And she was so happy when I revealed my gift to them.

I didn't date for more than three years after Moe, but the minute Landon came into my life, I finally understood the story my grandmother told me about how she met my grandfather. He is a partner at his law firm and loves making people happy. He makes me happy. As well as our eighteen-month-old twins, Logan and Landon Jr.

I feel happier about where I am in my life. I am about to enter my office when I get a call. It is from a correctional facility in Oregon. I have no idea who could possibly be in jail in Oregon.

"Hello."

"Hi. Hi, Crystal." And then I hear his voice, and instead of fear or hatred creeping up inside of me, I feel sorrow.

"Hello, Moe. So, you're in jail." Thank God for years of therapy. I never thought I could be this calm speaking with Moe again after everything he put me through.

I walk into my office and shut the door behind me.

"Yeah. Got caught up with drugs, and it's really serious this time."

There is an awkward silence.

"It's been nine years. Why are you calling me?" I ask.

"I—I should have done this sooner, but I have been too scared and did not know what to say."

I cannot help the scoff.

"I know that what I did to you was unforgivable. And I know it does not help to let you know, but I was diagnosed with Bipolar Disorder when I was a teenager. I preferred to deal with it using cocaine instead of my medicine.

"I know I hurt you, and I am not saying right now or anytime soon, but I just want you to know that I am sorry and hope you forgive me. I am really sorry for what I did to you. I am also reaching out to everyone I have hurt in the past. Which includes your mother and stepfather. Please let them know I am working to be better."

I hear a dial tone before I can even respond. I wait a moment for him to call back and say we got disconnected, but he doesn't. Thankfully. I'm not ready to have a conversation with him about that dark time in my life.

Not yet. I don't think I ever will.

And about forgiving Moe, *only time will tell*!

Epilogue
Therapy Continued: May 2022

"SO, DOC, THAT'S EVERYTHING. That's everything I can think of. What do you think?" I say to Dr. Andrews, feeling a bit relieved.

"I think that you did good, Crystal! I think that you are well aware of yourself and the things that have transpired throughout your life, and that is the first step—to accept what it is that you've been through," she answers.

"I just want to be the best version of myself for me and for my family. I know therapy has helped me with this quite a bit … but I know I have more work to do."

"What you are experiencing is natural. Healing isn't a linear process, so there will be times when you may feel as if you've wandered off your healing path and fallen into some shadows–

I cut her off, "I do, Doc. I have wandered off so much … then I always bounce back! But it seems like it's taking a while."

"That's good. As long as you are okay with knowing you'll take a few steps back at times. As humans, we unconsciously set expectations to heal, but there isn't a deadline for it, Crystal. You are only human, and you've already learned to stop minimizing your emotions. This happens over time when you do the work to cultivate and practice emotional intelligence. So, what you are doing is just allowing yourself to cry more tears and validating your emotions instead of getting rid of them. Managing them is the answer—and you are doing that. It's all a part of healing. The best thing here is that you acknowledge it all. It's okay for you to not feel okay all of the time. What we will focus on is how we can keep moving forward. What are some positive things that you think you can do to keep it pushing?" she asks.

"I guess making sure I'm not suppressing my emotions, keeping up with my positive thoughts, practicing self-care, and letting my feelings be my teacher to help guide my evolution."

"And that's all you need to keep doing! Don't forget to commend yourself for being dedicated to your healing. Have you forgiven yourself? Have you forgiven everyone from your past, including your mother, your father? and Moe? You have to forgive Moe too."

"I absolutely have forgiven myself and my mother. I'm still working on everyone else. I know that pain is part of my journey. I am not broken, and I am on Earth to learn and grow. *My soul is whole!*" I say with a smile pinned on my face.

"We will resume this conversation in two weeks. You have to forgive everyone else, too, Crystal, but we will work on it. Do you have any more questions for me?"

"No, ma'am. Thank you, Dr. Andrews. See you in two weeks!" I say as I get up and head toward the office door.

I stop and look at the Lion King portrait again for a moment before walking out. Thinking about Simba's journey, it warms my heart knowing that Simba still became the King of Pride Rock even after his uncle, Scar, tried doing everything he could to take that seat away from him. Luckily, his father, Mufasa, taught him to respect the Circle of Life and maintain a balance between predator and prey at an early age. I'm just like Simba—I persevered anyway!

Note From The Author

Thank you so much for spending time reading my book. If you enjoyed reading it, I would appreciate if you could:

Leave a short review on Amazon. Let me know what you thought. I read every review and they will help other readers discover my book.

Share it on social media. Help more people discover my story. Word-of-mouth is the best marketing for budding authors.

Connect with me. I would love to hear from you. Stop by my website at **www.thebravemethod.org** and subscribe to my newsletter for the latest updates.

Thank You!

Afterword

Given the immense number of possible worlds out there, the fictitious events that occurred in this novel have got to be true in at least one of the worlds, so perhaps it's not as fictitious as we imagine. *Right?*

Crystal's Method is a creative fictitious story; however, so much of it is based on events that occurred in my real life. When I was a young child, my relationship with my father was non-existent. Once I became an adolescent, he was no longer a resident of Detroit, where I live, but we were able to form a long-distance relationship. Just like many other long-distance relationships, it faded. Over the years, it would resurface, fade, resurface, fade, resurface, fade again and again. My personal belief is that part of a father's duty is to lead, provide, and protect their creations from the world. From childhood to adulthood, I was left with an inconsistent father and no leadership.

It was such a formative part of my growing years that it almost aligned with everything else. But sometimes, I catch myself wondering what my life would be like if he were 100% present. Would I have a better life? Don't get me wrong, the village—my mom, grandmothers, aunts, etc., did a great job raising me, but that will never measure up to a father's impact or a father-daughter relationship to me. And right before my eyes, in no time, most of the village had started to leave the earth.

I respect my mom so much for being so strong and courageous at such a young age. My current age, 31, is the age my mother was when my grandmother made her transition, and she was left to raise me and my uncle, who is a year younger than me, alone. That is strength, that is brave, that is heroic. Crystal's mother isn't an exact depiction of who my mother is, but a representation of so many other mothers in the world, some of whom I have encountered. My goal was to just put the reality of others' lives into perspective.

I lived with my grandmother for a big chunk of my childhood and had an attachment to her existence, so her transition was one of the worst pains I've ever felt. My great-grandmother was also a big part of my world. Although it has been nearly 20 years since they've left this earth, my memories with them never seem to diminish, and I have the same pain that I had on the days they left. Every day is still a struggle. I catch myself asking the same question that I ask myself about my father—would I have a better life if they hadn't left me so soon? These were Crystal's sentiments throughout the story about her life, and grandmother, who is both of my grandmothers, but combined.

We live our lives and come up with these plans for our lives, sometimes forgetting that it's God that is going to be leading our footsteps. In contrast, Crystal did not devise a plan and took the lemons that life threw at her. Although that is not ideal for most, it's how life happens for many people. While she wanted to give up plenty of times, she kept pushing. Sometimes the support from the people around us is exactly what we need to remind us of our strengths and to keep pushing through life—that's what worked for Crystal and me.

Was I as delicate and tender as Crystal? No. Was I as vulnerable as Crystal? Yes. People often misconstrue the realism of vulnerability and automatically associate it with weakness. There are several negative deep-seated emotions associated with being vulnerable when a person shows up in a situation, and the result isn't favorable. Can we all agree that putting yourself in a position to be susceptible to harm while being mindful that you aren't in control of the result is courageous? To do that time and time again is brave of anybody. Being vulnerable is one of my greatest strengths. It can be gratifying, or it can be vain. Unfortunately, it's not up to you.

It is difficult for those who've abandoned their vulnerability to appreciate love, warmth, and close bonds with others, as doing so prevents them from being their true authentic selves. When I yearned to receive love through an intimate relationship, I had a shift in awareness that allowed me to control my emotions by being aware of what my pain points were at the time. Once I entered the relationship that turned abusive, all barricades were down, and my heart was open. Of course, I was unaware of the toxicity and dangers coming my way. It took years to learn that it wasn't being weak that got me there either. My emotional response to my abuser could be thought about as a survival mechanism. Early on, there were many red flags; however, I had not been taught what the red flags were to be able to identify abuse or an abuser. It wasn't until it was too late that I learned what I was dealing with.

For me, healing has taken years of self-examinations, self-reflection, therapy, and more. And because I am healed, I am whole and complete. My experience also didn't shadow me. Human nature is greatly flawed, but I live in the realm of those flaws while still being able to be whole and my authentic self. While learning more about myself during my growth, I've encountered and witnessed many women in the same place I found myself in, dealing with the same abuse that I did, or even worse. I am here 9 years later with the ability to reflect on my experience comfortably and overtly. There are many barriers that women face in abusive relationships that have an advantage on their emotional response during that time. I understand …. Sure, I wrote this book to be entertaining and give you readers a good story, but the goal is also to help others understand that those barriers exist and helping others identify the red flags was critical for me.

Society has normalized so many negative cycles, domestic violence is one of them. In addition to many turning the other cheek, it is difficult for many victims to realize that they're being abused by their intimate partner, sometimes because of their family dynamics or other reasons. A way to help them identify the abuse is by increasing awareness and education. The closest woman to you could be experiencing abuse, and nobody would know it unless she knows what it is, and then decides to tell it. Unfortunately, it is normal for women to protect their partners; therefore, it stays a secret. This book was written to be a voice!

ACKNOWLEDGMENTS

First and foremost, I'd like to thank the Most High. Without God, none of this would be possible. Putting this book together has been a surreal process. It has been just as rewarding as it has been challenging. None of this would feel complete without the people in my life who have been there to support me and help me to the finish line. Thank you so much to everyone who has contributed to the birth of this project.

To all of my beta readers, thank you for dedicating time to my process and for your comprehensive feedback. Every one of your evaluations were valuable in my editing process. Thank you for helping to ensure that my story and message were as strong as possible.

To my editor, Chelsea, your editing skills are impeccable. Thank you for all of your feedback, guidance, suggestions, and ideas that helped structure my story. Thank you for all that you do. Brian, thank you for your talent and for bringing the main character to life on my cover. Kenney Lock, thank you for all your motivation, your thoughts, your ideas, your advice, your listening ear, your time, and your support. You are an amazing person.

Andrea, thank you for listening, always supporting me, having my back, and making sure I stayed on track with my goals. Stormee, thank you for your support, your pointers, and being there to listen. Things as simple as just listening to me vent my ideas to helping me decide on character names meant a lot to me during this process.

P. Hill, thank you for being the voice in my head that was my inspiration for changing my situation.

To my mother, thank you for teaching me to be strong before my real life had even begun. I thank you for letting me bump my own head; my experience wasn't in vain. Thank you for your unwavering support. I love you!

I will forever be grateful to my stepfather, who God sent to love my mom and me. You've filled several voids that many men aren't capable of doing. I love you for that.

A special thanks to Tyrone Hairston—my therapist/mentor! You are one of the best things that have happened to my life. Thank you for facilitating the behavioral changes I needed to make to ensure I successfully completed my book. Thank you for your direction. You've helped me to rid insecurities that were hindering me from reaching my full potential. You've helped me with self-understanding and self-acceptance, both needed to complete this book. You've taught me self-compassion, greater self-awareness, and more. These things will follow me throughout my life! I will forever be indebted to you.

To those being raised in abusive households and live their lives in fear and are voiceless. To those who have experienced abuse at the hands of an intimate partner. Thank you for reminding me of the significance of sharing such stories through creative writing. To every reader, if you are holding this book in your hands, thank you.

Lastly, I would like to thank myself! Not often enough do I give myself credit for accomplishing the things I have done throughout my life. Instead of waiting until I reach the end goal, I've learned to celebrate my wins, accomplishments, and progress along the way. So, before I reach "a million copies sold," I would like to pat myself on the back for doing the work it took to get there.

About the Author

Jaz Cyan is a serial entrepreneur and author of *Crystal's Method: A Domestic Abuse Novel.* After years of analyzing trends in abuse, Jaz has a subjective eloquent voice that is recognizable on her blog, where she writes about the importance of the community's support in domestic abuse awareness. Jaz has a BS in Criminal Justice and Criminology from Eastern Michigan University. When she is not absorbed in a professional project, she enjoys traveling to sandy beaches with blue water, spending time with her family and friends, and laughing so hard that she cries. Visit **www.thebravemethod.org** to see what Jaz Cyan is up to. Sign up to get exclusive insider material and deals.

www.instagram.com/thebravemethod
www.facebook.com/thebravemethod1
www.twitter.com/thebravemethod

Discussion Questions

1. "Daddy Issues" is a catchphrase that refers to the psychological term, father complex. Discuss how society has attempted to detach the phrase from men and ascribe it to only women. Discuss how a father complex can affect men and their adulthood.

2. We learn early in the novel that Crystal's father had abandoned her and her mom. At their young age, Crystal didn't know what "Daddy Issues" meant, but Nelly was more advanced and tried to attach that stigma to Crystal. Discuss Nelly's perspective on "Daddy Issues" as a child.

3. What were your opinions about women in abusive relationships before reading Crystal's Method? How did you come to form your opinions? Have your opinions changed?

4. Compare and contrast Crystal's relationship with her mother and her grandmother. How did her upbringing impact these relationships?

5. Crystal never told anyone about the bathroom incident with Sean. She says, "I don't even know if it is a thing." Discuss why Crystal might not have understood what happened to her.

6. Crystal remembers that Trisha had a busted lip in her first relationship with Sean. When Trisha starts dating Titus, Crystal only ponders about why her mother puts herself through the pain that she does. "I did not ask her where or how she got the bruised eye, just pulled her into the hug and let her cry it out. I tell her how much I love her, my heartbreaking as I watch her put her dark sunglasses back into place and force a smile on her face." Why do you think Crystal doesn't talk to her mother about her horrible relationships with these men? How does this affect Crystal?

7. Crystal's grandmother was the only nurturer in her life that she had an attachment to. How do you imagine her passing away affected Crystal as she transitioned from adolescence to adulthood?

8. After Crystal, Danielle, and Nelly graduate high school, during their discussion about some of their future plans for college and beyond, they fall into a group hug. "We stay like that for minutes. Enjoying the moment. Knowing that our entire lives are about to change and that we are taking different boats on uncharted waters. But I am very confident that I am always going to have these ladies in my corner. My own tribe." Why is this moment so important in Crystal's journey?

9. Justin seemed to understand that Crystal didn't want to have sex after their date, but Crystal couldn't come to grips with feeling like her experience with Sean had taken over her life. She goes back to the motel the next day to apologize and to have sex with Justin. Discuss her mindset at this point. Why did she feel she needed to apologize to him?

10. Crystal reiterated that she never felt as if Justin was the one she wanted to marry. Discuss her relationship with Justin up until it ended. Discuss the decisions she made in their relationship and how they could've possibly set the tone for her future relationships.

11. Throughout the story, Crystal's relationship with her mother is dysfunctional. Discuss the changes in their relationship. Their conversation in Crystal's dorm room quickly escalated when Crystal realized that she no longer wanted to be vulnerable at that moment. What do you think was the trigger that made her metamorphose into the daughter that evokes their negative past relationship? Trisha began trying to support Crystal during her transition to college. Why do you think Crystal rejects her efforts instead of accepting them? How do you think Trisha felt at this point?

12. After returning to Detroit and looking for Richard to apologize for what happened in the dorm room, he drove her home. "He would make a wonderful father, I say to myself as I watch him drive out of sight. For the first time in a long while, ever since my grandmother, I felt seen." Discuss the significance at this moment.

13. Crystal makes an exception to dating again when she meets Dre at the Ultimate Black Party. She then tells Deja that she isn't looking for something serious, but she'll appreciate dating him because he may be different than Justin since he's older. What is her current obvious approach while dating? What explains Crystal's lack of desire for attachment? What prevents people from wanting attachment in relationships?

14. Why did Crystal feel an instant connection to Moe after learning some of his background information?

15. How did Trisha and Richard's wedding influence Crystal?

16. Why doesn't Crystal want her mom to meet Moe? Why does she protect his character?

17. Crystal posts a picture of her and Moe on Facebook with a mushy caption. What role does social media play in relationships in today's society? Refer to the passage: "The post got a lot of comments and likes. And I have to admit that it made me feel good. I can almost imagine a lot of girls seeing the picture and reading my post and dying with envy. Moe is good-looking and attractive. Just walking down the street with him makes me feel special enough. I know it is vain and maybe stupid, but I don't care. I am going to enjoy this."

18. When Moe hits Crystal for the first time, what does she instantly think about?

19. Too deep into the relationship, Moe convinces Crystal to stop working at Cobras with plans to support her needs. Later, he falls short with money and can't support himself or Crystal. After learning that Moe can no longer provide a home for them, why do you think Crystal chooses to stay with and follow Moe instead of going back to live with her mother? Why do you think the author chooses to frame the ending of the novel with these scenes? How is this significant?

20. Consider Moe's abusive gestures: tracking Crystal's whereabouts, controlling her employment, invading Crystal's privacy by going through her phone, etc. What does each reveal about who Moe is? Why is Moe's behavior challenging for Crystal?

21. Given all of the conflict in Crystal and Moe's relationship, why do you think Crystal still chose to reach out to Dre when her car stopped on her in the middle of the road? Would you have reached out to Dre if you were in Crystal's shoes?

22. What challenges does Crystal face while at war with her own mind and staying with Moe even after she experiences the abuse?

23. Discuss Crystal's method on leaving her relationship with Moe.

24. Over time, what does Crystal learn about love and happiness? What life lessons do you think Crystal learned? What lessons did you learn from Crystal's life?

RESOURCES

If you or someone you know are a victim of Domestic Violence, there are several resources ready and available to support. Check out the listed resources.

National Domestic Violence Hotline
PO Box 90249
Austin, Texas 78709
Hotline: 1-800-799-7233
TTY Line: 1-800-787-3224
Text: "START" to 88788
https://www.thehotline.org/

HAVEN
801 Vanguard Drive
Pontiac, Mi 48341
24-HR Crisis & Support: 248-334-1274
Toll-Free Crisis Line: 877-922-1274
TTY Line: 248-972-2540
https://www.haven-oakland.org/

MaleSurvivor
https://malesurvivor.org/

Parents for Megan's Law and the Crime Victims Center
Hotline: 1(888)ASK-PFML

https://www.parentsformeganslaw.org/
pfmeganslaw@aol.com

The Brave Method
24225 W 9 Mile Rd
Ste. 140 #3034
Southfield, MI 48033
https://www.thebravemethod.org
thebravemethod@gmail.com

Department of Defense ("DoD") Safe Helpline
1220 L Street, NW
Suite 500
Washington, DC 20005
Hotline: 877-995-5247
https://www.safehelpline.org/

Cyber Civil Rights Initiative
Hotline: 844-878-CCRI (2274)
https://cybercivilrights.org/

Safe Haven Shelters - The Humane Society of the United States
1255 23rd St. NW, Suite 450
Washington, DC 20037
202-452-1100 or 866-720-2676
https://www.humanesociety.org/all-our-fights/fighting-animal-cruelty-and-neglect

American Psychological Association (APA) Locator
https://locator.apa.org/

National Alliance on Mental Illness
Hotline: (M-F, 10am-6pm EST) 800-950-6264
https://www.nami.org/Find-Support

The National Coalition of Anti-Violence Programs (NCAVP)
Hotline: (212) 714-1141
https://avp.org/ncavp/
info@ncavp.org

credit.org
Hotline: 1 (800) 431-8157
https://credit.org/services/

OTHER BOOKS TO READ

Set Boundaries, Find Peace: A Guide to Reclaiming Yourself by Nedra Glover Tawwab

How to Do the Work: Recognize Your Patterns, Heal from Your Past, and Create Your Self by Dr. Nicole LePera

What Happened to You?: Conversations on Trauma, Resilience, and Healing by Oprah Winfrey and Bruce D. Perry

Jump: Take the Leap of Faith to Achieve Your Life of Abundance: by Steve Harvey

Relentless: From Good to Great to Unstoppable by Tim S. Grover

Can't Hurt Me: Master Your Mind and Defy the Odds by David Goggins

www.ingramcontent.com/pod-product-compliance
Lightning Source LLC
Chambersburg PA
CBHW020034310726
48970CB00007B/2256